Aaliyah's

Secret

Writer's Block Publications

P.O. Box 640
Jonesboro, GA 30237

ISBN-13: 978-0615775456

ISBN-10: 0615775454

Cover Design by: The Lyricist Firm

Editor-Kiara Reynolds

Manufactured in the United States of America

Aaliyah's Secret

Nikki B

Author's Bio

Nikki B was born in Atlanta, Ga. She has three brothers and one sister who is also an author.

Nikki started writing at a very young age. She wants anything more than to share her passion for writing with the world.

She is a young author and hopes to continue to bring you the best of novels throughout the years.

Special Thanks

I will like to take time out to thank my mom and dad, my nieces Tamaya , Tynisha, Asia, and my brothers for supporting me.

I would like to thank God for blessing me with the passion and drive to become a writer.

Last, I would like to thank my sister Veronica Meek for taking me under her wing and welcoming me into the Writer's Block family.

Nikki B

P*ROLOGUE*

I will remember October 10, 2011, forever. It was the day that one of the most dreadful secrets I carried around came into play. I'm going to tell you my story so you will understand the choices I made, and the secrets I held.

"Aaliyah wake up." I heard my mother yell.

I tossed and turned while hitting my pillow. She always wakes me up at 6:30 in the morning because I have to walk to school. I hate getting up this early because I still have 2 hours to get ready for school. I would go back to sleep if it wasn't for our maid, Mary, who would usually let me get a 15 extra minutes of sleep, but today she made sure I got right up after my mother left.

My father would have woken me up if he was home, but he had a business meeting today, so he left early. Mary had my uniform already laid out for me. I got out of bed and went to the bathroom to take a shower. When I was in the shower I remembered that it was my boyfriend's brother's birthday.

My boyfriend is Charles Parker and his brother is Samson, but we call him Sam for short. Sam is turning 20 years old, but he still around least 18. He sometimes freaks me out. Every time I leave my house to go to school he would be looking out of his window or standing outside staring at me. I asked Charles what was up with his brother, but he never gave me an answer. So I never asked him that question again.

When I got out of the shower I

walked down the stairs leading to the 4th floor looking for Mary; that's when I saw someone looking into our living room window. I moved closer to the window and was able to see who it was as they dashed down the street.

I ran to the front door yelling.

"I'm getting sick of you spying on me Sam."

While I was standing there watching him, Mary walked to the door.

"Aaliyah why are you out here in nothing but a towel and house shoes?"

"Because Sam was spying on me again." I yelled.

"This is the 10th time this week. What is wrong with that boy anyway?"

"I really don't know. Charles didn't want to tell me, but if he keeps doing what he's doing he's going to end up hurting somebody."

I couldn't remember what I had to ask Mary so I headed back up to my room and put on my uniform. After I finished pressing my hair I ran back down stairs.

I went into the kitchen where I found Martin fixing breakfast *(which he does every morning for no reason)*. I don't know why because he doesn't work for my parents. I guess he does it because he's unemployed now and has nothing better to do. When he sees me he smiles and says the same thing each morning.

"Good morning, Aaliyah. How are you?"

"This is not a good morning Martin, but I'm doing fine, and how are you?"

"I'm great little lady now that you're here. I have your favorite."

He always knows what I like for breakfast, which is eggs (extra cheesy), butter milk pancakes with butter and syrup, hash browns, or two pieces of ham, and a slice of toast with jelly. Today I told him I didn't want anything because I wasn't feeling too good.

He looked at me sideways "OK then if you say so."

I smiled at him; I knew what he was doing. So to make him happy I grabbed a pancake and a piece of ham, rolled it together, and ate it on the way back to the living room. I grabbed my stuff and told them I'll see them later as I ran out the front door.

Nikki B

CHAPTER 1

It was about 7:50, when I left my house unaware that I was being followed. When I walked down the street to my friend's house I found out that Maya had already left. I was pissed off because we always walk to school together. I made it down a few more blocks when I heard a noise behind me. That's when I start to panic. I walked a little faster, and now I was scared because I didn't know who it was. When I saw the shadow I was sure that it was a man.

So I walked faster, then he walked faster. When I turned onto the next block

I felt a hand grab my arm as the other one covered my mouth.

He pulled me into an alley before saying, "If you dare scream, I will cut your tongue out."

I was so scared; I couldn't even move my body. He pulled out a pocket knife and started to cut my clothing. As they fell down I was left with nothing on but my bra. When he started to unfastened it I begged him to stop. I started to cry as he kissed me and moved his hands down between my legs.

I felt so dirty. I started to shake as his hand moved higher and higher up my leg. I tried to scream, but nothing came out. He pushed me hard down to the ground. While he stood there unzipping his pants I tried to get up and run, but he dropped down on top of me. He fell right between my legs. I tried to close them, but it was too late.

No matter how hard I tried to fight it didn't stop him from pushing his self–

inside of me. The more he pushed the more it hurt.

I cried out. "Please stop it hurts, it hurts."

He looked at me. "I'm almost done."

As the minutes passed I couldn't take it anymore. I tried to yell again that's when he put his hand back over my mouth. A few seconds later he screams out.

Once he removed his hand I yelled, "Please get off me!"

The pain was unbearable so I passed out a few seconds later.

When I woke up, I knew it was too late to go to school. I couldn't go anyway with my uniform looking like this. There wasn't anything left to do but grab my things and go back home.

I got up slowly looking around for my things. I tried to put my clothes back together as best I could before I walked away. When I tried to walk my legs start trembling. I hadn't gotten farther then two blocks when I saw a black sports car speeding up the street, and it stopped right in front of me. I was frozen in place waiting to see who was going to get out. As the doors slowly opened, I feared that it might be him, but I was happy to see that it was only Martin and Mary.

When they approached me I saw the worried looks on their faces. Mary was the first to say something.

"Aaliyah, what in the world happened to your clothes?" She said as she ran over to me.

I was so scared that my body started to shake as soon as she touched me.

I started to yelled. "NO!NO! Please stop! I'm begging you! Please stop!"

Mary saw how scared I was and tried to stop me from yelling. I was so weak and before I knew it I passed out again. The last thing I saw was Martin pulling out a blanket putting it over my half naked body. I didn't even feel when he carefully picked me up, and laid me down on his back seat.

The next time I woke up, I was in my bedroom. I don't know how long I laid there, but I didn't try to move until I heard Mary coming up the stairs.

"Aaliyah what happened to you this morning?"

I looked down at my legs and saw cut marks as if he had been cutting me to scare me.

"I don't want to talk about it right now."

From the look on her face I knew she wasn't going to let it go, but she left the room saying she'd return later.

I got up out the bed slowly. I was still in pain. Tears came to my eyes as I walked to my closet and pulled out another uniform and laid it on the bed. I went into the bathroom, took another shower. When I was finished I asked Martin to take me to school. He looked me in my eyes before saying that it was too early to go back to school after being attacked.

Nikki B

CHAPTER 2

On Monday morning I over slept because Mary wasn't here to wake me. When I got to school I found out that I only missed 15 minutes of homeroom. That didn't bother me too much because all we do is talk and play around. So while I am kind of happy, inside I am still full of fear.

As I walked into the room the teacher asked why I was late. I had to come up with something fast. When I was about to say something, the bell started to ring. I thought to myself "Yes! Saved by the bell".

The rest of school went by pretty

fast which was good. I only had one more class to go to and that was gym.

Once class started I asked if I could sit out because I wasn't feeling well, but just like always Ms. Hamhawk said, "No".

Well I decided that I was going to take my sweet time to get ready. When I got inside the locker room I realized I didn't bring any sweat pants, all I had with me was a red T-shirt with writing on it saying; "All The Girls Want To Be Like Me" and some shorts that stopped at my knees. I didn't want all the other kids seeing my legs all cut up. I knew that they would ask me what happened.

So to hide my scars, I only put on my shirt and went back out on the gym floor. When Ms. Hamhawk saw me, she told me to go back into the locker room and put on my shorts.

I asked slowly, "Do I have to? I mean it's really cold in here and all I have is shorts. I'm sure I'll freeze to death."

Ms. Hamhawk looks me up and

down before she said out loud.

"I don't care if your legs turn black and blue, go and change into your proper gym clothes or else I will call your mother."

The last thing I wanted her to do was to call my mom. My mom works really hard and I don't want to make her mad with the problems I'm having. So I turned around and headed back to the locker room.

On my way to the locker room, I heard footsteps and a hand grabbed my shoulder. I jumped and turned around to see that it was only Ms. Hamhawk which was kinda weird because she only follows her bad students into the locker room.

"Why are you following me?"

She looked me up and down again. I was about to walk off until she pulled me back and whispered into my ear.

"What happened to you last week, Aaliyah. Don't you even try to lie because I do know your maid, Mary Washington?"

I looked into her ice blue eyes and realized that I wasn't leaving this locker room until I told her the truth. So not to make thing worse *(then they already were)* I decided to speak, but before I could get anything out I felt myself about to throw up. I ran to the trash can and everything I had for lunch came up.

When I was done Ms. Hamhawk asked, "Aaliyah are you pregnant."

In a quick second I yelled out, "NO! WHY WOULD I BE PREGNANT?!"

Ms. Hamhawk left out the locker room and returned with a pass to the nurse's office.

"Go to the nurse's office and get yourself tested to see if you are. I just want you to know that if you are."

She handed me the pass and told me to put my uniform back on.

The bell rang as soon as I made it to the office letting everyone know it was time to go home, but I continued on to the back where the nurse's office was

16

located.

"Hello Ms. Hamhawk told me to come and see you."

"Okay is something wrong?"

"I wasn't feeling too well in gym and I was throwing up so Ms. Hamhawk sent me to you."

"Okay lay down over there for a moment."

I hated being in the nurse's office because she asked too many personal questions.

"Ok honey, now give me the real reason why are you here?" she asked with her big rosy color cheeks.

"I need a pregnancy test." I said low and shy like.

She made an unusual face at me and went in the back room. When she returned she handed me a stick like thing.

"All you have to do is pee on this and it will give your result in words okay. Now go use the restroom."

I hopped off the bed and went into

the restroom. When I walked back into room the nurse looked up from her paper she was reading.

"So what did it say?" She asked me while smiling.

I looked down at the result then back up at her and a single tear came down my cheek.

I said with tears of joy, "I'm not pregnant, the test is negative."

*C*hapter 3

A few minutes later the late bell sounded and the last of the kids rushed from their classes. The nurse looked at me before she walked back into the back room. After she returned she handed me two more pregnancy tests.

"Listen honey, I don't know if you're really pregnant or not, but just to be sure check and see a couple more times. I want you to take these and use one of them on the 15th and use the other on the 25th. You got that sweetie?"

I was still crying, but gave her a

soft yes. I was wondering how I was going to tell my mom that I got raped. The worst part was that I don't know who raped me, or who would even try. Now I'm more worried about whether or not I'm pregnant.

As I walked home, I made a list of all the good and bad things that came from having a baby. The good is that I would have a reason for not having my homework, not being in school some days, or why I'm falling asleep in class. Also, I could sit out in gym and don't have to sit in those uncomfortable desks and chair for 9 months.

The bad part about having a baby at sixteen is I might not be able to go to college. I wouldn't be able to get any sleep, or to be able go to hardly any parties with my friends any more. And not too many boys want to date a girl with a baby. What really is going to be hard for me is not knowing if my mom would say if I could keep the baby or not.

When I got home I put my list in my jacket pocket, and greeted my mom with a hug and kiss as I walked through the door. I sat my bag down and decided to talk to my mom for a while. I listened as she talked about what was happening on her job and how her boss was thinking about giving her a raise.

"Momma that's good. How much more money you'll be getting?"

She smiled as she rubbed my cheek. "It would be a thousand dollar raise. That means I will be making at least six thousand now."

I was so happy for my mother that I wasn't going to spoil her happiness, not today anyway. I got up, heading toward the door so I could go upstairs to my bedroom, but the sound of my mother's voice stopped me.

"Was the test negative or positive, Aaliyah?"

I was shocked. I couldn't believe that she knew about me getting tested.

"How do you know that I got tested?"

She looked at me with disappointment in her eyes.

"The nurse called me after you left the school. Aaliyah, please tell me that you're not having unprotected sex."

"Momma, no; I have never had unprotected sex with anyone, but there is something you need to know."

She jumped up out of her seat and ran across the room; grabbed me by my neck and pushed me up to the wall.

"After all that I give to you! You go out and have unprotected sex!"

I grabbed my momma's hand. "Momma please let me go, I can't breathe."

She jerked me from the wall and threw me to the ground.

"Why would you make the same mistake I did, Aaliyah?"

I held my neck as I tried to pull in air.

"Momma I didn't go have sex."

"If you didn't have sex than why did you go get tested, Aaliyah?"

I started to cry. "I....I....was raped."

My mother emotion changed really quickly.

"Oh baby, I'm.... I'm sorry. I didn't know." She got down on the floor and held my hand. "Do you know who did it?"

I dropped my head down. "No. Well I don't know who did it, but I do have a few thoughts on who it might be; I'm not saying who until I know if I'm pregnant or not. Ok."

She looked at me as she cried, but said yes. We both got off the floor, and she pulled me close and gave me a hug.

"We will work things out baby I promise. Now go on upstairs. We will talk about this more later."

That night I had a dream about Sam and Charles. It was back when they were little kids. In my dream Sam was 12 and Charles was 8 years old. I could see them playing inside of their house. A few minutes later their front door opened, and a man walked inside. It was their stepfather. He went over to Sam and grabbed him by his neck pulling him into another room, and then started reaching for his pants.

Sam said while moving away. "Daddy, I don't want to do that."

At that moment I realized that Sam had been sexually abused. It was so terrible. I had dreams like this before but this is the first time that I believe that I may be psychic, because every time I dreamed something out of place like that it always comes true.

So the first thing I did when I woke up was call Charles. When I looked at the clock it was 1:50 in the morning. We talked for a second then I ask him to meet me at the park around 2:00. From the sound of his voice he wasn't happy about it. But when I got to the park he was already there.

"Babe, what was so important that made you wake me up?"

"What were you dreaming about?"

"I was dreaming of you course. You know you're my baby."

"I know I said that I wasn't going to ask about it anymore, but I have to know...." I cleared my throat, "Did Sam ever get sexually abused by your step-father?"

He looked at me in shock.

"How did you know about that?"

I wasn't sure how to tell him so I pulled him over to the swing set and told him about the dream I had.
oHe was silent for a minute.

"He was abused by him, but to tell you the truth Jordan wasn't even interested in Sam. He would do some of the same things to me like take pictures, and sometimes take baths with me. He tried things with me, things he hadn't tried with anyone else. Then it was getting too hard to hide the scars he left on my body. One day he came into the house drunk, as usual, and calling for me. I was about to go until Sam told me to hide. So I did. I never did stand up for myself. I always ran and let Sam take all the abuse; now Sam is in some deep trouble, because I heard that he raped some girl on her way to school."

I stopped him right there.

"Wait, Sam raped a girl on her way to school?"

Charles looked away from me before he answered.

"Yes, and don't asked me why or if I know the girl, because I don't."

"Charles, I would like to call Sam. Can I call him from your phone?"

He looked at me but handed me the phone, but as it started to ring I handed it back to him.

"Charles do me a favor and ask him if he likes me."

"But why?" He asked looking confused.

"You'll see. Just do it please." I begged him.

We could hear Sam yelling on the phone.

"Hello...Hello who is this?"

"Sup bro, I'm just wanted to know if you like Aaliyah?"

"Man, do you know what time it is and why you want to know that; I thought that was your girl."

I looked over at Charles telling him to go on.

"I just want to know because I'm thinking about bringing her home so both of us can have some fun with her."

It was quiet for a while, and that's when Sam said something that surprised both of us.

"I don't like her, I LOVE her, and I had my fill of her, so you can have your way with her now. Good night."

"Night big bro talk to you tomorrow.

When Charles hung up he took his

27

phone and threw it across the park. I heard the sound of it when it landed hard on the cement.

I knew that he was upset because, my brother Kevin had given him that phone before he died last year. He gave it to him for his birthday. That was the only thing he had of Kevin. It was even hard for him to use his phone after my brother's death.

He fell down on the ground, and put his head on his knees and began to cry. I sat down beside him but was too scared to touch him.

When I finally found the strength to make my move, he looked over at me.

"Aaliyah, can you please braid my hair that always seem to calm me down."

I looked at his long beautiful hair "Of course anything for you baby."

We got up and walked over to the swings. When he sat down in front of me I started to run my fingers through his hair. I did about 10 braids and then sat down on the swing beside him.

He touched his head, "Thank you babe you know I never asked you where you learned to braid like this."

"My mom used to own a hair salon so she taught me."

He reached over and grabbed the swing which made the swing jerk a little to the side. I turned to him and that's when he kissed me. We stayed like that for a few minute and when he finally stopped kissing me, I knew I wanted more.

I wanted more of his kisses; more of his hugs, and most importantly, more of him. I grabbed his shirt and kissed him. He wrapped his arms around me and pulled my closer. We didn't stop until we needed air.

"Aaliyah, I was wondering ...."

"Wondering what?"

He looked away. "How about I show you a sample of what I was thinking about."

29

He pulled up my skirt, and rubbed my legs.

"Oh you really want to do that Charles? I mean with me?"

"Yes I do."

Then he started to kiss me again. We laid down on the ground. I knew that we were both nervous so we begin to laugh for a while. He looked in my eyes smiling then he kissed me again.

We were both so into it that I reached down and started to touch him. He reached under my skirt and started to touch me too. I couldn't help myself. I took off my jacket, and laid it down so I can lie onto of it; and then I lifted up my skirt.

It was cold out here so I wrapped my arms around myself to keep warm. When I looked at Charles I knew seeing me like this was turning him on.

"Aaliyah you are so beautiful. Are you sure you want to go through with this?"

"My answer is the same as before."

He nodded his head, reached out for my hand; then he pulled me into his lap. Slowly he joined us by lifting me up and placing me down on him. The further down he pushed me the more it hurt.

That's when I started to panic and screamed out. "Pull it out! Pull it out!"

"I'm sorry babe but you feel so good. I can't hold myself any longer. I gave you the chance to back down, but instead you wanted to go through with it."

He lifted me up and placed me on my jacket, but I didn't want him to leave so I reached up and wrapped my arms around his neck.

He took that as a sign to continue and I didn't find it in my heart to stop him this time. The faster he went the more it hurt.

I was glad when it was over, but I couldn't help but pray that if I was pregnant that maybe the baby would be his.

31

Nikki B

*C*hapter 4

After we were done we laid there and talked about all the fun we used to have. I even reminded Charles about what Kevin said to him when we started dating. I remember it like it was yesterday. It was when Sam and Charles were staying with us because their mother was in jail for shooting their step-dad.

He ended up dying; not by their mother but by his other wife. To tell you the true I don't understand why she was the one who went to jail; when he was the one that was abusing them I would never understand that.

When their mother went to court she used a lawyer who was a close friend to their step-dad. He made her case sound like an act of murder when it was really an act of self-defense. The judge sentenced her to 20 years in jail.

Since they couldn't get in touch any of their family the judge asked Sam and Charles did they know anyone that would take care of them. When they said no the judge was about to send them to a foster home until my mother and father stepped up and said that they would take care of them.

My family went through a long progress before they were allowed custody. At that time I was 10 years old, Sam was 14, and Charles was 11; that's when our relationship started to change.

Not long after that Charles came and asked if I would be his girlfriend so I said yes. At that time I told my big brother everything. So the first thing I did was pull him aside and told him what Charles asked me.

He walked over to Charles and told him to follow him. Charles looked back at me with a scared look in his eyes. But I smiled at him before he went upstairs.

"Charles do you know that you're one lucky dude. I don't have to tell you that you have a great girl here; she's a girl that will smile even when she's hurt, just to make you smile. Remember this one little thing. This is my little sister, and if you hurt her. I will hurt you."

"Mister you have nothing to worry about because my mom raised me to be a good boy."

Kevin smiled and hugged Charles and said to him in a whisper. "Welcome to the family."

That was when Sam changed toward me, he was upset about the fact that I was dating his brother and not him. I told him that I can be his girlfriend too. He just gave me a little kiss on the cheek.

"No because you are my brother's girl and I don't want to take you away from him but, I will always wait for you because I will always love you."

That was so long ago and at that moment I saw how innocent I used to be back then. How could I be both of their girlfriends? When I said that Charles started to laugh, and then he looked away.

"Aaliyah was you serious about what you said about you wanting the baby to be mine?"

"Yes, don't you know that you're my heart, my soul, and my world? If you would have left me, I would have died. Baby, I LOVE YOU!"

I guess somewhere in that statement I started to cry. Charles hated it when I cried. He would always say that he can't see my beautiful smile when I did that. He pulled some tissues out of his pocket, and began to clean my face.

I started to get cold so I got up to put my jacket back on. He looked at me, while he zipped up his pants. He reached for my hand and we walked back to my house.

I was a little sore and he saw the look of pain on my face.

"Are you okay baby?"

"Yes, I'm just sore that's all."

"I'm going to help you inside then."

"It's okay I can make it."

"No you can't you can hardly walk. What make you think you can go up the stairs without falling."

I pulled one of his braids hard just to show him I was serious, but in the end he won. As we were walking up the staircase, we weren't counting on getting caught by Mary and Martin who was just getting home from their date. Charles dashed up the stairs into my room and shut the door.

As listen I heard footsteps coming up the stairs and they were heading towards my door.

Charles whispered. "Where do you

want me to hide?"

I pointed to the closet as I jumped into my bed. I wait for a while trying to see if someone was going to open my room door. Something told me that it couldn't be Mary or Martin because they never come to my room before it's time for me to get up for school. I started to get scared.

Charles walked out of the closet and came by the side of my bed.

"Did you know that your mother and father weren't home?" He asked me.

"No. I did not know. How did you know that?"

"There was no car in the drive way and I don't think Mary nor Martin are here either."

I can tell that Charles had a very uneasy feeling about this also.

"Something fishy is going on and I want to find out." I said as I got out of the bed.

I walked to my drawer and pulled out

my red mini shorts and Charles's old football jersey.

"You still have that?" He asked.

"Yes, I love this jersey."

The jersey was a little smaller on me now, but it still fit and that's all that matters.

He walked over to me and gave me a kiss softly on my cheek. I turned to him, and kissed him back.

"Please don't go. I don't want you to get hurt. If that happens I would never forgive myself."

I saw that he was about to protest. I kissed him on his cheek and walked out the door into the hall. I walked down the stairs to the 3rd floor which is where I heard the noise. Then I heard the door open and close.

"Aaliyah, I know you are in there bring your butt out here."

Once I heard his voice I knew who it was.

I yelled out. "Sam, what are you

doing in my house?"

"Aaliyah I had to come. I have to ask you something."

He walked up and grabbed me. I jerked away and ended up falling. I got on my knees and started to crawl away, but didn't get that far, because he grabbed my leg. I started to scream as he pulled me back.

Then he started to laugh.

"Damn girl you look sexy in your night clothes. I might go for another round."

*C*hapter 5

I screamed as loud as I could and wished that Charles would hear me. Sam stated to rub my leg.

"I can't believe I made that many scars on your pretty little legs. I was so into it that I didn't realize it. You must have been enjoying it because you didn't say anything."

"Sam please let me go."

He released my legs and sat down.

"I have something to ask you. I just want to know if you told on me. Please answer honestly."

"No I don't tell on a friend even if

41

they did get me pregnant."

He leaned back looking surprised. "Pregnant!" He repeated to himself. "Aaliyah you are pregnant?"

"I'm not sure."

I put my hand on my stomach. He looked at me softly before reaching out and touched my stomach.

"If so then that's my baby. I promise you I will be a good father."

I didn't know how to tell him that there was a strong chance that the baby wasn't his.

"Yes it might be."

He hugged me, and even though he raped me he was still my friend and I loved him like a brother. His hug felt the same as if I was hugging Kevin.

In the mist of all that was happening I didn't see Charles come down the stairs. He had heard everything but to learn that the baby might be Sam's was too much for him to handle. He ran past us and out of the house. From the look on his face I knew the truth of the situation finally hit him that his brother had raped his girlfriend and maybe gotten her pregnant.

***

I haven't seen Charles in two weeks. I was worried about our relationship, because we never went this long without talking to one another.

I looked out my window hoping that I would get to see or talk to him sometime soon. I don't know if I talked him up or what, but there he was running up the hill in front of my house,

I jumped up and ran downstairs trying to catch up to him. I was glad that he had only run to the river two blocks from my house. He was sitting by the river. I walked over to him and wrapped my hands around his neck. I didn't say anything I just wanted to hold him.

"I can't believe it. Are you sure the

test was negative?"

I kissed his cheek, "I don't really know if I'm pregnant or not, but I had to tell him something so he would let go of my leg. Plus he needed to understand what he did to me."

He pulled away from me.

"Aaliyah you didn't have to say nothing to him. He was wrong for what he did and you act like it didn't matter that you might be pregnant. You know you can be stupid sometimes." He jumped up and grabbed me by my arm. "Well I love you too much to let you have a baby with him. So if this baby ain't mine now, or if you aren't pregnant trust me there will be a baby after I get finish with you tonight."

I was speechless.

"I know I hurt you the first time, but today I'm going to take my time and be gentle. Are you sure you can handle this?" He said as he kissed me on the neck.

"Yea I can handle anything as long as I don't lose you."

He made me so happy I had no choice but to kiss him.

"It will be different this time once we get going. You can't stop me in the middle of it like before, because I don't want to mess up my flow."

"You been hanging around Roc and Ray haven't you?" I asked laughing at him.

"Now that's none of your business. But if you must know yes because I needed some money."

"You need money for what?"

"I had to get you this." He pulled out a little black box that was wrapped in a red ribbon. "Here open it."

"What is it?"

"Just open it Aaliyah."

I pulled the ribbon off and opened the box. My eyes got big

"Oh my God...Oh my God!" I started to scream.

I looked down again and couldn't believe that I was looking at a diamond ring.

I watched as he got down on one knee. I couldn't help but cover my mouth as I held back my tears as he took my hand in his.

"Aaliyah Morgan Jackson, will you do me the honor of making me the happiest man on Earth by becoming my wife?"

"Yes, oh Charles yes!"

As he slid the ring on my finger I began to cry again.

"Babe why are you crying?"

"Because if I am pregnant with Sam's baby, how could I marry you? Would you want to take care of his baby?"

"Who would you rather have a baby with? Me or Sam?"

"You already know the answer to that. I want your baby."

The way he looked at me he saw that maybe I was unsure about this whole thing after he turned his back on me.

"Aaliyah I want to ask you something."

"What? What is it?"

"You know that you was my first love right?"

"Yes I know just as you are mine."

"You was my first everything, Aaliyah. You were my first friend, my first crush, my first girlfriend, my first love, and my first lover! If being with Sam is what you want then go get him; who am I to stand between you and your wishes."

I could not believe what I just heard.

"Is that what you believe that I would want to be with him instead of you? Is that what you think? You know what Charles, you make me sick. You never believe a word I say. I have been your girlfriend for years. You think that I wanted him to raped me and get me pregnant? Charles if anything I want to have your baby not his."

He lowered his head. "You are a liar! If you didn't want to have his baby then why did you let him touch you?"

I was shocked that he would even think that I wanted Sam in anyway.

"You're stupid butt must not heard me when I said that I WAS RAPED! What kind of boyfriend thinks that his girlfriend wants to sleep with another man? Now I see why women find other men because they are not getting any love from their own man. Charles Antonio Parker, YOU ARE NOTHING BUT A WUSSY."

Before I knew it Charles had punched me in my face. He hit me so hard that I fell down to ground. Once again I was shocked that day; because he have never hit me before nor have he ever raised his voice at me.

Chapter 6

When I touched my cheek I started to taste blood. I could feel my face starting to swell. I had pain shooting though my head. It wasn't long before my tears start to fall.

He turned around when he heard me crying. It was almost like he couldn't face me. His back was to me; it just broke my heart to see how he hated me for what happened to me. When he turned back to me I looked up and saw tears in his eyes.

"Aaliyah, babe are you okay?"

I was scared so I flinched when he touched me.

"Please, please! Don't hit me again!"

I got up and ran. I knew then that my relationship with Charles would never be the same.

I don't know why I ran to Charles house, but he and Sam were my best friends. I didn't have anyone else to turn too. Once Sam saw my face he knew just what happened to me.

"Did Charles do that to you?"

"Yes, but…"

Sam interrupted me. "There is no but don't you make excuses for him."

"You can't get mad Sam; look what you did to me too. Both of y'all are just alike."

He didn't say anything else because Charles walked inside the house. He stopped short when he saw me standing there talking to Sam.

Sam didn't say anything just walked up to him and punched him in the face.

"You fool do you know what you have just done?"

Charles stood there holding the side of his face. "And what have I done?"

"You broke your promise to Kevin. Plus you didn't have a reason to be putting your hands on her; boy do you know what her parents would do if they saw her looking like that?" Same didn't give him a chance to response. "I guess you don't because your ass is stupid."

That only made Charles angry so he punched Sam in the mouth.

"I know one thing you're not the one to be calling people stupid after what you did to her. Plus why should I care about what happens to her. She wants you now! She always wanted you!"

Sam smiled before he punched Charles in the stomach which brought him down to his knees.

"Maybe now you will listen to what someone is trying to your butt." Charles was trying to get back up but he kicked him in the stomach this time. "You're dumb! Aaliyah is in love with you not me.

Do you even understand what she was saying? She said that that baby may not be mine. She wants that baby to yours. Please don't be upset with her. She loves you too much to let that baby break y'all up. She even told me that if this baby is mine that she will raise it with you, and I want what's best for her."

Once Sam finished talking, Charles went crazy. He ran upstairs to his room and pulled out the silver box that Kevin told him to hold. Inside of it was a gun. He took it out and heading back downstairs; then pointed it towards Sam.

"Since we were little you stole everything from me. You stole my money, my toys, my food, and now you are trying to steal my girlfriend. What kind of brother would do something like that? I trusted you and you raped my girlfriend. What kind of mess is that?"

"I don't know man; I don't know why I do things like that."

Sam finally broke down. They have

been doing each other wrong ever since they were young. He knew that it wasn't anything he could do to solve the problems they had over night.

"I'm sorry Charles I never thought about the things that I took from you; it's just that Aaliyah is sexy and we knew her ever since we were little. I couldn't let her go, but if killing me would correct the wrong that I have done then do it."

Charles didn't say anything as he pulled the trigger.

I couldn't believe my eyes as all of this played out in front of me. I love both of them and one of them could be the father of my baby. How could I let this go this far? I tried to run in between them. When I heard the sound of the gun going off I screamed; not because I was afraid, but because instead of the bullet hitting Sam, it hit me.

Once Charles realized what he did, he ran over to me.

"Oh my God Aaliyah I'm so sorry I

53

didn't mean to hurt you." He said through his tears.

"Call 911 please." I cried out.

Sam pulled out his cell and it wasn't long before he called out his address.

Charles was looking at me trying to see where I had been shot, and he showed a sign of relief when he saw that I was hit in the leg.

Once Sam got off the phone I saw that he wasn't too happy about me taking a bullet for him. He just stood there watching me.

"Why would did you do that?" Sam asked.

"Because I am pregnant, and I don't want to raise this baby alone."

They both said. "YOU ARE!!!! HOW DO YOU KNOW????"

I was in pain but I had to let them know.

"I was supposed to have my period a week ago but it hasn't come. I had only one pregnancy test left, so I took the test to see if I was and this time it came back positive. Since I don't know who the father is, I couldn't let this happen."

I can't tell if they are happy or scared but I can feel that they are worried about me and the baby.

I closed my eyes and tried to relax a little before help arrived. I don't know what we are going to tell people so we have to come up with something. My leg started to feel like it was on fire and then slowly my sight began to fade until darkness took over.

I had to be dreaming because I saw Kevin standing across the living room. I called his name but it was like he didn't hear me. Oh how I missed him.

My dream begins to change and now we're at Kevin's funeral. I try to wake up but my dream changes again. This time we're at my Aunt Patricia's funeral."

More and more flashes of my past come and go. I am lost in pain until I feel myself coming to again. I heard voices around me, and I knew then that help had arrived.

*C*hapter 7

Wh?hen I opened my eyes again I was safely inside a hospital room. I looked around hoping to see Sam or Charles but they were nowhere to be seen. Maybe that was a good thing. I don't want them putting two and two together and finding out that Charles was the one that shot me.

I moaned when I tried to move. My mom was asleep but she jumped up after hearing me.

"I'm okay mom I was just trying to sit up."

She smiled and sat down on the

side of my bed.

"Aaliyah what happened over there with Charles and Sam?"

"Nothing, mom it was a mistake that's all."

"How in the world you call getting shot a mistake?"

"Where are they anyway?"

"I guess they're at home. What you need to be doing is worrying about you and that baby you're carrying. So when were you going to tell me about being pregnant?"

"Mom I just took the last test the nurse gave me. I was going to tell you. I swear that I was."

"I believe you baby. I still want to know how you got shot and who did it."

"I'm tired right now, mom maybe we could talk about it later."

"Okay I'm going to go home for a little while. Would you like for me to bring you something to eat back?"

"Yes, I would love that. Thanks

mom."

I closed my eyes as she walked out of the room. I couldn't help but think about Charles and Sam. Where were they and why weren't they here with me. I turned and faced the window and saw that it was raining outside. The last thing I said before I went to sleep was, "Charles where are you?"

I slept for about two hours and Charles or Sam still weren't here. I was getting upset but mostly I was hurt because they were the reason I'm lying in this hospital bed in the first place. My door opened and in walked the brothers. I didn't smile even though I was glad to see them. I'm not going to let them know that their being here meant that much to me.

Sam was the first to say something. I laid there watching him as he walked toward the bed,

"Why do you look so sad? What's on your mind?"

I wish it was more than just him and

Charles not being here but I also had something else weighing heavy on my heart. I didn't want to say anything about it but who else do I have to talk to other than them.

"Kevin."

"What about Kevin?"

"It was something that he said before he died."

"What did he say that has you thinking about it now?"

"I don't know if I should say anything."

"Aaliyah if something is bothering you just tell us." Charles said as he jumped into the conversation.

"Well I don't really know where to start."

"How about at the beginning." Sam replied.

"Okay, on the day Kevin got killed, he made me promise not to tell anyone about what happened."

"What happened...why?" Charles

said as he took a seat.

"He had his reasons Charles."

"Okay what else."

"Like I was saying he said something while he was dying that I need to make something up."

"Make something up; I still do not understanding why." Sam said.

"The day someone shot up Kevin's apartment; I was there at the time. Kevin pushed me inside the closet and made me hide. I did what he said before whoever was shooting came inside the apartment.

"You were there when Kevin got killed?" Charles asked.

"Yes I was there. I'm sorry I didn't tell you. The only other people who knew are my parents." No one said anything else so I continued to tell them what was on my mind. "I just don't understand how he could ask his little sister to make up lies about someone dying, and the worst part about it all is that I did it. I lied about my own brother's death. How could I do that?"

I broke down at that moment. I wrapped my arms around myself trying to feel some comfort. Charles grabbed my hands and Sam started to wipe away my tears.

"It will be okay." Charles said.

"If what you told us a lie than how did he really die?" Sam asked.

"Please tell us." Charles held my hands a little tighter.

I closed my eyes. "Ok. I will tell you." I said as another round of tears rolled down my face. "The day before Kevin died; He took me to his friend Chuck's house. He told Chuck that he needed me to stay with him while he went to pick you two up from your friend's house. So Chuck agreed. Kevin left and about 2 minutes after he pulled off, a man came and knocked on Chuck's door. When he looked and saw who it was, he came back and handed me his cell phone saying. "Call your brother and say the black bird is in the wrong nest. He will know what it means." Then he took my hand and pushed me under one of the cabinets in the kitchen. So I did what Chuck told me. I called my brother and told him what he had said. Kevin sounded upset and mad. Then he told me to stay put and don't move from where Chuck had put me, he will be back there shortly. So I hung up the phone and stayed balled up under that cabinet."

"Wow is that all that happened?" Sam asked.

"No there's more. Are you sure you want to hear this?"

"Yes I'm sure!" They both said out loud.

"The cabinet door opened and I felt someone's hand around my neck pulling me from my hiding place. I was so scared. I looked up and saw Kevin. Then I heard the man say "if you move any closer I will blow her brains out." That's when I started to scream, "Kevin! Please help me

I'm scared." Kevin looked at me and said " Don't worry I got your back but I need you to do what I showed you. Ok?" I grabbed Charles' hand again for comfort "I nodded and started to kick the man. That's when he lost his balance and fell. I ran towards Kevin unaware that the man was pointing his gun at me. When I reached Kevin, he pushed me as soon as the shot was fired. I watched as Kevin fell holding his arm. When I saw what happened to Kevin I was so mad that I grabbed Kevin's gun."

"You did what! Come on Aaliyah are you serious?" Sam said while looking from me to Charles.

"I grabbed his gun. I could hear Kevin yelling; "Aaliyah what are you doing......NOOOOOOOOOOOOO!" But I wasn't listening to him I was so mad that he shot my brother that I shot the man in the head. Kevin grabbed the gun from me. I was shaking so bad so Kevin grabbed me and we left. You just don't know how scared I was that day."

I couldn't even look them in the face. I haven't told anyone about that day. I buried my face into Sam's chest, Charles held on to my hand tighter than ever.

Sam pats me on my back. "There, there, everything is going to be alright ok."

I don't know what made me tell them or why the day came back to hurt me but it did. Looking at the gun Charles held in his hands brought back one of the worst days of my life.

Nikki B

*C*hapter 8

Charles looked over at us. "Finish!"
I could tell that he was upset so I leaned over to kiss him, but he just moved his head. "He's so stubborn!" I said to myself. "You know the rest of the story, but after Kevin picked you two up we went back home. He said that he told y'all that I wasn't feeling good."

"So all of this is the truth?"

I looked over at Charles as he nodded. "I remember Sam and I both stayed near your bed that whole day. We never left. There was no reason to leave sleeping beauty alone without any protection."

I laughed then continued with the story.

"The next day, the day that he died, Kevin decided that it would be best for me to stay at home he said that I needed time to take in all that happened that day. I really didn't want him to leave me because I was so happy to spend time with him. I never got to spend much time with him. I begged him to let me go so he told me to put on some clothes and took me to the park. When he arrived back to his apartment, we ran into another man who stopped us on our way inside of his apartment.

"Kevin Damien Jackson?" he said in a bold voice. "Yes" Kevin said as the front door of the apartment flew open, but before he could turn around he took me and pushed me inside the door." I knew I needed to hide, just like the day before. I knew that something was wrong. I heard Kevin run inside and close the door. "Go hide in the closet Aaliyah!" He said in a low voice. As soon as I opened the closet door I heard the man shooting inside the apartment. I started to cry. I just knew that he had shot my brother. When I didn't hear anything else I opened the closet and walked out and there was Kevin laying there on the floor covered in blood. The man was still standing there looking down at him. I looked up and asked him why he took my brother away from me. In a cold voice he replied. "That nigga never should have gotten my sister pregnant and denied her baby. God she was only 15 years old and he's an ass grown man. The man looked at me one last time before he put the gun to his head and killed himself. I never felt ashamed of my brother before that day."

"Aaliyah, I'm sorry. Did you even know that guy?" Sam asked.

"Yes I knew him as soon as he removed his hat; it was Percus. I asked him while he was dying."Wha....why....why did you shot my brother? He was supposed to be your best friend. "He never got a chance to answer before his eyes closed.

I looked at Charles and saw tears fell down onto his shirt. I reached my hand up and rubbed his cheek.

"What's wrong?

"Get off of me."

"Wow...."

He cuts me off. "It's hurts."

"What hurts?"

"It's kind of messed up to know that the only person that you looked up to as a positive example of an older brother was just as messed up as my own brother, but that's not was hurting me. What was hurting me was the fact the only person that I can trusted lied to me and kept the truth hidden from me. That's what hurts. How am I supposed to marry you if you keep secrets like that from me? How am I supposed to love and trust you if you lie to me? How am I supposed to know if you are telling me the truth or not when you say that you love me? How, Aaliyah? How?" Charles asked with so much pain in his voice.

I couldn't bear the fact that Charles was questioning my love for him.

"You would know whether or not I love you.... I wouldn't be carrying your baby if I didn't love you. I would not allow you to have sex with me even if I didn't love you, I would not keep your old school jersey if I didn't love you. I wouldn't consider your feelings every time a male friend asks me to go out if I didn't love you, and I wouldn't be laying here trying to reason with you if I didn't love you. But most important, I wouldn't still be holding on to the place saver that you gave me until you got me a real ring."

My heart was completely broken. I could not bear this sorrow anymore. I knew what I had to do now and even though I knew it was going to affect both of us, it had to be done.

Nikki B

Chapter 9

I was so upset and so hurt. I couldn't believe he had said all of that. How could he doubt me after all this time that we've been together.

"Charles, for six years I have been with you and in all that time I trusted in you, but I can't take any more of this. I'm sorry but...." I began to cry, "I've got to end this relationship."

Charles looked at me with tearful eyes. "But.... Aaliyah.... why?"

"I can't handle this anymore. You accused me of cheating on you, you hit me, and now you are questioning my love for you."

Charles looked at me and then at Sam. I turned my back on him. Not only do I have the pain of my perfect love being broken, but the pain of being shot as well.

I didn't say anything else I just laid there listening as he starts talking to Sam.

"I blew it this time didn't I?" Sam nodded. "How am I supposed to fix this. I mean I never knew that she would be this unhappy with me. Should I have acted a little more caring? Should I have acted a little more thoughtful? What should I have done?"

"After 6 years you still don't know what Kevin was trying to tell you that day you and Aaliyah fell out?"

"No man not a clue."

"What he was trying to say is that no matter what Aaliyah or any girl looks on the outside it does not compare to what's on the inside. Under all that makeup and hair there is a sign that says handle with care. You just have to know how she wanted to but treated. You feel me?"

"Yea I feel you, but how am I supposed to get her back now?"

Sam looked up. "Show her that you care, show her that you love her for her and not for anything else, show her that she is the center of your world and that you can't live without her, but most importantly show her that you can change, because that is what's got you into this mess. That is what's going to get you out." For the first time in their life they actually listened to each other.

***

Three months passed and I haven't spoken to or seen Charles. Every now and again I would see Sam. I was still hurt and I didn't know how to deal with the fact that I told him most of my secrets. My phone started to ring and when I looked at the caller ID I saw that it was from Charles, so I just let it ring.

"You know you should really answer that boy calls or else you going to mess around and lose him for good." My mom said.

"I'm not about to answer that fool's calls.

"Well okay since you won't talk to him maybe you could start talking to me. I'm still waiting to find out who raped you. Do you remember who it was?"

"No not yet." I lied.

My mom and I ended up going to a pregnancy yoga class together later that day. Not long after I found out that I was pregnant she found out that she was also. It was a really big shocker to both me and my father. I don't think that he expected to have two pregnant women in the house.

When we got home I was tired so I ate dinner and climbed into bed, and I didn't wake until I heard the sound of my cell ringing around 1: 45 in the morning.

"Hello?"

"Aaliyah thank God you picked up this time."

"Charles, why are you calling me at this time of the morning?"

"Please don't hang up. I got something real important to tell you. It's about Sam."

That's when I heard the uneasy tone of his voice. "What about Sam?"

"He is in jail."

"WHAT!?"

I must have yelled really loud because seconds later my mom came busting into my room.

"Ok. Thank you, Charles." I said as I hung up the phone.

Nikki B

Chapter 10

I sat up in bed and looked at my mom. Why would Sam get arrested? Did someone find out that he raped me?

"What's wrong dear?" She said as she closed my door. "

"Charles just told me that Sam is in jail."

"Oh so they finally came and got him then. That's good." She said happily.

"What do you mean they finally got him? Mom what did you do?"

"I read your diary and had that monster arrested." She said proudly.

I couldn't believe what she had

79

done. I was so mad at her.

My mom sat down. "There, there baby doll, you have nothing to worry about. That monster is gone now. He will never hurt you again."

I looked up at her. "Monster, the only monster here is you, you're a heartless person. How could you go through my diary and read all my personal information?"

"You watch your mouth while you're talking to me young lady. I'm the type of mother that wanted answers which her daughter didn't see fit to give. I was just looking out for you sweetie. I didn't want him to hurt you like he already did. I care about you too much to let you get hurt. I already lost one child. I don't want to lose another."

I pulled away from her. "How dare you tell that lie and say that you cared about me? You didn't care about me when Kevin was living. It was always about him. You only cared about your golden child.

You're treating me like this because you can't forgive yourself for his death. You were trying to replace him so you can have some form of confront. You're an evil hearted woman."

She slapped me.

"How can you say those things Aaliyah? I have given you everything. The best clothes, the best schools, the best everything, and this is how you repay me by calling me out of my name. You must be out of your damn mind because I am your mother not the other way around."

I rubbed my cheek and got up. There was no way I was going to take that pregnant or not. I'm not going to let no old woman hit me and get away with it.

"You're not about to start hitting me again! I'm not scared of you anymore."

She looked at me with tears in her eyes. It looks like she wanted to say something but instead she turned and walked away.

The next morning I went

downstairs and saw my mom, Mary, and Martin were all in the kitchen.

"Hi baby cake!" Martin said as soon as I walked in.

I waved at him because I was still tired. Mary and momma were silent and the only thing that was playing was the television. It was on the news and what was being talked about was shocking. As I sat there watching I couldn't believe my eyes. They were showing Sam being pulled away by the police. He wasn't struggling or anything. He stopped and looked at the camera.

"I am so sorry, Aaliyah. I know what I did to you was wrong and I do not blame you or your mother for reporting me to the police. I just want to let you know that I love you so much that it was hurting my heart to see you suffer with trying to keep my secret. Just remember that I LOVE YOU too much to hurt you."

With that the police took him away. My heart was filled with emotion and my eyes were filled with tears. At that very moment, I began to feel Sam's love for me.

My momma said as she looked at the T.V. "Who is he to be filling my baby head with lies? He doesn't really love her. He's just like all the other men. They have their way with you and then leave you."

I gave her a sharp look and walk out of the room. In the back of my mind all I could say was, "Shut up! You can't get mad at my relationship with him because you never had that kind of relationship with anybody accept daddy." I ran out of the kitchen with tears running down my face.

Nikki B

*C*hapter 11

I didn't get farther than the living room. How could my mother understand how I feel about both Charles and Sam? I love both of them. Would she even understand that? I lay across the sofa, listening to what was happening on in the kitchen.

"Emma, you know you treating that girl wrong." Mary said.

Emma laughs. "Who are you to tell me about how I treat my child when you don't have one of your own?"

"If you were paying attention to her you would have known as soon as Martin and I did 3 months ago that that child had been raped. Plus I have 3 children, my oldest, David is a doctor, my second, Nicole is a singer, I think you have heard some of her songs, and my youngest, Jeremy is still in college studying to become a doctor just like his brother. You would have known that if you bothered to talk to me and really get to know me. So you can't say I don't have a say in how to raise kids when I have been raising your kids for years. You think your life is so good, have you ever decided to ask your daughter how her life is, or have you been too busy with all the finer things in life?"

The kitchen got silent so I guess my mom was surprised to hear that Mary had a family. The only thing that troubled me was that fact that Mary was living here with us instead of with her own family. I guess my mother must have been thinking that too.

"I know what you thinking, you evil witch, and the reason why I'm here and not with my babies is because they have their own lives to live. They've families of their own, and I didn't want to be alone. Your husband is a wonderful man and when he came to me and asked me to watch over your kids I felt honored. Now I see why he asked me to be here; you do nothing but use that man as your own little game piece. You know something, my husband left me and my kids when my youngest was 5 years old, and he never looked back. You have a husband that stayed with you no matter what. Yeah he may have left once but he came back and me and you both know it wasn't because of you, but for the kids."

When Mary stopped, I heard my mom laugh. It sounded a little wicked to me.

"You need to wipe that stupid smile off your face. Oh you think I didn't know about the time that your husband left you. Oh trust, I know everything that goes on in this house. There is not one secret that you can keep from me. I know it all, best believe that."

I watched as my mom walked out the kitchen. Then I heard Martin and Mary singing "A change gonna come."

I ran up the stairs to my room and called Ms. Parker she was a close family friend of both my parents and Charles and Sam's mother. She was really happy to speak to me after so long and it was good to talk to her. After a few minutes of conversation I asked her if she could take me to see Sam at the jail.

"Of course baby anything for you.

I got dressed and was waiting out front when she pulled up to the house around 3:45 that afternoon. I ran up to her and gave her a big bear hug as soon as she stepped out the car.

"Hello baby. How have you been?" she asked as she hugged me back.

"I have been doing fine." I responded.

We were listening to music playing

when Ms. Parker asked, "What happen between you and Charles?"

"It's just that he changed. I mean I love him very much, but he started to question my love for him, and I couldn't take it no more."

"Since he has been living with me, all he does is sit in his room looking at pictures of you, and listen to sad songs all day. But there are some good things too, like his have grades improved and, he's helping out around the house. Plus he's being a lot nicer to my little Malik. You know he's 9 years old and in the 4th grade now."

"Really, I haven't seen him in years; that's great. What school is he going to?"

She smiled at me and said, "James Wallace. Isn't that school named after your grandfather or uncle?"

I nodded. "My grandfather; it was because of my Aunt Patty, my mom, my Uncle John, and my Uncle Ben. That's good that he attends that school."

"I wish when I get that old that my family would name a school after me."

Ms. Parker laughs for a second and turned the radio up. "Oh I love this song."

"Me too." I said and started to sing along with her. I haven't felt this good in months.

*C*hapter 12

We sung all the way to the jail; I'm not going to lie once we arrived I kind of got scared. As we walked down the sidewalk leading into the building some big, ugly man was yelling out improper comments. Our whole way up we heard.

"Hey sexy!"

"Can I get some of that?"

Ms. Parker and I walked side by side. She looked over at me and said, "Don't listen to those creeps; they're nothing but dirty pigs that's why I can't stand coming here."

I laughed at her and kept walking until I saw a boy no older than Sam sitting at a table through one of the window.

Then out of the blue some guy grabbed me by my arm. It scared me for a moment until I heard Charles voice.

"Hey get your hands off my girl."

I smiled because even after I broke his heart, he still saw me as his girl.

"Hey Aaliyah"

"Hey Charles I came as soon as I could."

"You didn't have to come here."

"Yes I did; it's because of my mother that he's in here."

"I don't want to talk about that. So how are you and how did you get here?"

"Ms. Parker brought me."

"That's good."

"I'm good and so is the baby." I said as I placed my hand on my little baby bump.

He looked down and smiled. "You do know that no matter what you are my girl, my wife, and my life I can't let anything happen to you baby."

"Please, forgive me for everything; these past three months without you have been a living hell. I need you so that I can be who I am. I need you as much as you need me. I guess what I'm trying to say is... I want you back or I'll just die."

"Aaliyah you are the best thing that ever happened to me and I never did let you go. To tell you the truth I told myself that me and you never stop being together but at some point I started to think that you would never except me back again."

"I want to thank you for coming here and trying to see Sam."

"I couldn't sit around while Sam's in here and not try to see him or I didn't want him to think that he doesn't have a friend in the world either, because he would always have me."

"If you could forgive Sam, would you be able to forgive me as well."

"Oh Charles I forgive you. I couldn't live without y'all and I don't want to."

"So that mean you will take me back." He asked looking me dead in my eyes.

"Oh yes baby I will take you back."

"You know that night I called you I wanted to beg you to take me back then, but once I saw Sam on the news I knew that I had to wait on that and let you know about Sam first."

For the first time in three months my heart got warmer and I even felt there was something more between me and Charles now. Something deeper than what we had before.

"I will never let you go Aaliyah. You are like a rare gem that I want all to myself."

I kissed him.

"I can't let you go neither because you are the oxygen that I need to breathe so without you I would die."

We talked until Ms. Parker walked

up.

"Aaliyah are you alright?" She asked as she looked from Charles and me.

"Yes I'm okay we been talking trying to work things out."

"Yes she's okay she has me to protect her." Charles said as they all started to walk toward the visiting area.

"Are you coming home for dinner tonight?"

"Don't I always. How are you doing Mr. Andrew?"

"Ain't nothing just been working hard as usual. Well, well, well, who is this beautiful young lady?"

"I'm Aaliyah."

We talked all the way to the front desk and the woman behind the desk looked up at us. She had a big small on her face once she saw Charles. It looks like I seen hearts form in her eyes.

"Hello, Mr. Charles. Are you here to see your brother or me?" The front desk clerk said.

"Well, Tracy, as you can see I'm here with my girlfriend you know my future wife and....."

He was cut off by someone screaming his name while running full speed toward him. She jumped on him making him lose his balance and fall.

"Hello babe. I knew you couldn't stay away."

I looked down at him and put my hands on my hips.

"Hayley, can you please get off of me. What are you doing here?"

She looked at him and then over at me, "Awww. Hey Aaliyah! Still acting stuck up."

"Hayley, still looking for a man?"

Man I can't stand the ground she walks on.The only thing that was going through my mind was to pull her by those two little things she calls pigtails.

"Oh I'm here to see my dad, but he didn't want my mom to see him today." She said with smile on her face. "Plus I'm kind of glad that I came because I didn't know that my boo was going to be here too."

"For the last time, Hayley, we are not dating. I broke up with you hours ago. I knew that it wasn't you that I wanted. You were just a tool that I was using to keep my mind off of my one true love, but it wasn't working."

"So I see that you don't care for me anymore, Charlie well that's okay because I going to show you what you're missing out on if you stay with that. She can't give you want I can." She said to him while unbuttoning her shirt.

She grabbed his hands and started putting them under her shirt like we wasn't out here in public.

"I'm about to beat your ass." I said as I punched her in the face.

I was really mad and I wanted to kill her.

Charles pulled me off of her. "Calm down, babe." He said with a scared look on his face. "Look she may have a big butt and pretty tits but what she don't have is what you do have; my heart, my soul, my child, but most importantly, me. Ok."

"The next time you jump on my baby's dad, I going to beat your ass up under this jail." I unzipped my jacket and showed off my belly. "You're lucky I'm pregnant."

So what if I looked like a balloon; but when Charles saw the size of my belly, he got down on his knees and placed his hands on it and gave it a kiss.

"OMG. You look so big." he said.

Ms. Parker and Andrew walked over to us and looked at me closely. "Oh honey, you are big I think you may be having twins."

I was amazed because my family has a history of twins and triples. "Now wouldn'tt that be a surprised."

*C*hapter 13

After the fight up front Tracy, was nice enough to let us still visit Sam. She said since it was slow no one even notice what happen. Charles already came here like three or four times since Sam's been locked up, so he pretty much had memorized his way to Sam's visiting area.

"I can't get over how creepy it looks in here."

"We'll be at the visiting area in a minute."

"Ok I hope it doesn't look as bad as this"

"It isn't that bad." He said with a slight smile.

"Good I'm happy to hear that."

Ms. Parker was following close behind, still talking to Andrew who was also watching over the inmates.

"Here we are." Charles said as we walked into the visiting area.

Sam was sitting with his head down at one of the tables. "Sam is that you?"

Sam slowly rose up his head and looked over at us.

"Yea it's me. Hey there baby girl." He said with a smile.

I was so happy to see him. "Oh Sam you look like you just got hit by a car. What have they done to you in here?"

"I don't want to talk about it?"

I looked at him and he had tears in his eyes and I felt so bad for him.

"Aaliyah now I know how ..."

I cut Sam off. "Please don't say anymore."

Charles grabbed my hand and told me everything that went down since Sam had been in jail.

"It brought back some very unwanted moments that I had hidden away from the world; even from myself." Sam said while holding back tears. "They left some scars here and there, but I...." Sam stopped for a second. "It hurts. It hurts really badly. That brought it all back. It reminds me of him."

I couldn't take it anymore it was too much to hear. My eyes began to water and it was getting hard to look at Sam without seeing that sad and scared little boy I saw back when we were so young. He was always sad and quiet.

"Sam I'm so sorry about this. I wish I never wrote that it was you that raped me, and I wish that my mother would have never read my diary. I wish that none of this has ever happened."

Sam reached out his hand. "You are ruining a beautiful face. Please stop crying because knowing these people; I would be lucky if I get out of here alive because these men don't play about people hurting kids. The only thing I want to remember is your sweet smile smiling at me."

I started to blush and placed my hands on my stomach. "Sam think about you're niece or nephew. They need of their uncle."

"Wow Aaliyah! You are getting big lil mama." he said while rubbing my stomach.

"Yeah I know we were talking about that earlier. It might be twins. We aren't sure right now." For the first time during our visit Sam smiled.

I got back home around 9 that night and my mom weren't happy about that either.

"Aaliyah, where have you been?"

I didn't even waste my time talking to her but walked up the stairs to my bedroom.

"Didn't I just ask you a question?"

I didn't feel like arguing with her tonight so I just told her what she wanted to know.

"Aaliyah you didn't go see that boy did you? Don't you know that you are making things worse by going to see him? My God it's like sending him a message that reads, 'Come get me I'm available'."

She was going on and on about going to see Sam.

"MOM, would you please SHUT UP! My God I can't even go to sleep without you talking about where I been." I said as I climbed into bed.

I saw that she wasn't happy about that at all, but left out of my room without any more questions. That night I slept really well and didn't have a care in the world because I was too happy to let anything ruin my good mood. I was finally back with Charles and that's all that matters.

Nikki B

*C*hapter 14

I'm about five months pregnant now but I look like I'm getting ready to pop. My mother is also entering in her fifth month.

Monday had come and I got up to go to school and was confronted by a lot of people wondering how many months I am now; with all the attention I kind of enjoyed being pregnant. It took me a minute to get all of my missing assignments turned in that I miss when I first found out I was pregnant. It wasn't long before I got my spot back on the "Principle's List.

In the middle of changing classes, I saw Charles walking down the hall toward me.

"Hey baby. Don't you have class on the other side of the school?"

"Yeah, but I came to walk you to your class."

While we were standing there talking one of the students' walked up and handed me a note.

"What is it Aaliyah?"

"It's a note from the Principal's office."

"A note; what does it say?"

I opened it up and started to read.

"It says that the principal wants to see us."

"Does it say why?" Charles asks as he grabbed the note out of my hands.

"No it doesn't. So come on let's get this over with." I said while grabbing his hand.

We walked to the office still holding hands. When we walked inside we saw the Principal, and my mother waiting for us in the office doorway.

"Hello Charles and Aaliyah, how are you today?"

I looked at my mother and she was wearing her evil face. I can't wait to see what trick she had up her sleeves.

"Aaliyah, it has come to my attention that you're pregnant, correct?" The principal asked.

"I think you already know the answer so why are you asking me that stupid question? Do you all think that just because I am pregnant that I'm different from the other students?"

My mother looked at me and rolled her eyes. Then turned and looked at Charles.

"Charles, you are the father correct?"

"Yes ma'am.", Charles said with a smile.

I was happy to see that he was handling himself better than I expected when it came to dealing with my mom.

The principal took that moment to step in the conversation.

"Well it looks like you'll have to add a new class onto your schedules if you want to graduate on time."

Charles didn't like the sound of at that.

"Why is that!"

I held his hand a little bit tighter and told him to calm down because getting mad wasn't going to do anything but get him kicked out of school.

"You missed a lot of days lately and in order to graduate you need to add this class. Taking this class will give you the points you need to graduate. Either you take it after school or during the summer as part of summer school course."

"Okay. What I have to do because I'm not going to summer school and sure not coming back here next year."

"It's not just you. It's mandatory that any student that gets pregnant has to take a parenting course."

"How much does this class cost?" Charles asked.

My mother replied. "That has been taken care of this morning. I paid for the class for both of you."

"What this class about?" I asked looking at the principal.

"It teaches you all that you would need to know on how to take care of a baby."

I listened to her talk and it made sense. I did miss a lot of days and taking this class would make sure I had all my credits, when it's time for me to finish school.

"Alright but is this going to infer with our regular classes?"

"No it's just a class to help you prepare for parenthood since you're going to be teen parents."

We talked a little more and then she released us back to our classes, but I wanted to talk to my mother before she left.

"Mom, I want to thank you for trying to help Charles and I prepare for everything. I just want to say; thanks for caring." Then I gave her a hug.

"Oh, Aaliyah I just wanted you to know that you don't have to go through this alone and that I'm always here for you."

"No, mom I did. I know I been hard to get along with lately and I'm sorry for that too."

"It's okay, baby. Now go on to class we will talk when you get home."

Charles waited for me by the door and I could still hear my mom talking to the principal when we walked out.

*C*hapter 15

Charles walked me back to class and we didn't see each other again until the end of school. I was told that Hayley was talking about me but my girl Maya got to her before she tried to fight me.

"Man, Hayley is a hoe. They should have named her Harlot!" Maya told me, Charles, and our other friend Tina.

I busted out laughing while Tina and Charles looked at each other confused.

"I don't get it. I mean Harlot sounds like a cute name." Tina said.

111

"Yea, if they named her Harlot then she would think that she was even prettier or something." Charles said.

"It's funny because Harlot really means hoe." Maya stated.

"Yea or in medieval times, a harlot was known as a prostitute. At least I think it was in medieval times. Hmm, who cares, it still means prostitute." I said.

We laughed and talked along the way home. When we reached Maya's house; we stood out front and made sure she made it inside safely.

After she went inside, we walked a little farther past her house and that's when we heard a familiar voice.

"Hey Aaliyah, want me to carry your books?"

Tina, Charles, and I looked with shock on their faces.

"YES, it's me Liyah darling."

I was so surprised and it stopped me in my tracks when I realized who it was. Only two people call me 'Liyah

Darling' and that's Sam and.....

"Daniel. How is my sexy baby!" yelled Tina.

I laughed and grab onto Charles arm. It had been a while since I heard her yell something like.

"I already told you⋯. I DON'T LIKE YOU." he said as he walked over to us.

Daniel was wearing a white V−neck sweater with a purple under shirt, black pants, and black shoes.

"Dude you look gay as hell? Why did Sasha let you out of the house looking like that?" Charles yelled as he put his arm around my waist.

A round of laughter spread through the whole group.

"He looks good to me, standing there looking like a big chocolate bunny in clothes." Tina said as she ran up and hugged him.

"Get off of me you evil little witch." Daniel said.

I couldn't help but laugh. Charles

was laughing at how Daniel was trying to keep Tina's hands off of him. We were so busy laughing at them that no one saw Maya.

"Daniel you CREEPPPPPP!" Maya said while throwing an empty condom packet down in front of him.

He jumped back not knowing what it was that she threw at him.

"What did I do!?"

"You were having sex in my room again. I told you if you want to have people over then you need to clean up your nasty room."

Daniel didn't say anything as he looked down at the open condom packet lying by his feet.

"I'm telling momma this time. I'm tired of letting you get away with this."

Maya turned and walked away. Daniel didn't move at first but when he saw Maya pull out her cell phone he took off after her.

"Got to go y'all."

Daniel said laughing as he ran to catch up with his sister.

Nikki B

*C*hapter 16

My dad would be coming home from New York in about two months. I couldn't wait because I wanted him home before his grandchildren were due. He called us a few times and said that he couldn't wait to get home. I know this was hard on my mom too because she had been getting on my nerves lately, and I'm at the point where I am about to rip her heart out.

I mainly sat in my room on my computer, talking to my friend Diana on Facebook. She was so happy to hear I was having twins and that she would be coming to see me sometime this year. I told her I was looking forward to it and logged off.

I started to feel sleepy, but decided to go outside and enjoy the fresh April air, and that's when I saw him. My eyes went wide and everything about this moment seemed crazy to me. I couldn't believe that I was looking at Kevin.

I was so happy to see my brother again so I had to run up to him and hug him.

"Oh...My...God. KEVIN!!!! OH MY God, KEVIN. YOU ARE BACK. I MISSED YOU SOOOOOO MUCH!" I couldn't help but cry because I was trying to figure out if this real.

"Hey there little sis. How you been doing?"

His smile was warm and his hands were gentle. I missed my brother's gentle touch, and his warm embrace. I missed everything about him. I began to cry and my tears started to wet the front of his shirt so he handed me a tissue.

"Why are you here? Did you come back from the dead?" I asked him.

"Naw. l just stopped by to see how my little sister was doing. I wish I was still here with you so I could see my niece and nephew."

I looked at him and wondered how he knew the sex of my babies, so I asked.

"I was showed your future and also Momma's to, but you have to stop treating momma that way. You see Aaliyah, your ending fits you. A good ending for a good person, but I can't tell you how it will end. That part is up to you. I know that Momma is beginning to annoy you but she is just being her."

He stopped talking as I looked at him. Then he laughed that soft laugh again.

"Man, if I had a nickel for every time momma got on my last nerve, I would be rich."

That made me smile. Then I started

to hear the sounds of bells and he looked at me with a sad look. I knew then that it was time for him to go.

"Oh looks like they're calling me back home. Well, Goodbye Aaliyah, and before I forget, I want you to go and do one last favor for me. Could you go to Percus house and tell his sister that I forgive her, and if I was her brother I would have done the same thing." He kissed my forehead and gently placed a piece of paper inside my hand.

"Bye, Butterfly."

I woke up with tears running down my face. "Bye brother of mine."

I didn't even know that I had fallen asleep.

***

For the last two months I had that same dream over and over again, but this time something was different. When I woke up, it was 7:30 at night. I was now seven months pregnant. I sat up in bed and a piece of paper fell out of my hand and into my lap.

I opened the paper and it was a letter and inside the letter was a note that had numbers written on it: 05-15-35.

"What is this? I said to myself.

There was only one way to find out and that is to read it.

Dear Aaliyah,

My dear sweet sister, Aaliyah.

Time has nothing on you. I just can't believe that my little sister has grown into a beautiful young woman, but I also can't believe that you're pregnant either. I know that you would do things a little different than our mom, because you know how it feels when a mother favors one child over the other one. Mom was never the best at being a mother but I hope that you will be the best mother to your babies.

I remember how you used to treat your dolls and yes including the messed up doll Auntie Patty gave you for your 4th birthday. You were only 4 years old, acting like a mother to those dolls. It always put a smile on your face to say "Don't worry baby. Momma's got you." That was your favorite line when you were little. Anyway, it was good seeing you Aaliyah my beautiful little sister. Until we meet again, Farewell

Signed,
Kevin Damien Jackson

P.S. The numbers are a code for my secret safe in my room. The safe is located behind the wall on the left side of my bed just tap the wall if it sounds hollow that's where the safe is and don't let mom see you or she will swear down that whatever is in the safe is hers. Take whatever you like. I love you my sweet little sister and remember big brother *loves you.*

I got kind of emotional when I read the letter. So it took me a moment before I got up off of the bed and walked out of my room. I stood in the hallway and listened to see if anyone was at home. Just to be on the safe side, I took the letter and placed it inside my pocket before I walked downstairs.

Momma was in her bedroom staring at a family picture back when Kevin was alive. I stood there for a second and smiled at the photo because Kevin had a silly look on his face. I was about 4 years old holding on to daddy's hand and momma was looking down laughing at us in the photo.

"She really does miss the old days."

I heard Martin say from behind me. I guess he knew what I was about to say because he cut me off with that same off the wall smile he always used.

"She told me several times that you

all was a good family then it all went wrong the first time your daddy walked out."

"No, it all went bad the day momma cheated on daddy with her co-worker. The baby she is carrying is not dads anyways and she knows it. She was throwing up food a month before daddy came back from his business trip in December so she must have gotten pregnant right when I did. Momma is nothing more than a slut, but she will always be my mother." I said I walked off heading on down the hall.

Martin closed my mother's door and followed behind me.

"Aaliyah, how do you know that the baby isn't your father's?"

I stopped and turned towards him.

"Cause I seen them. That's right don't look so shocked."

"Seen them where?"

"Here."

"You didn't see them here."

"Yes I did. I saw them having sex in one of the guest rooms."

"I don't believe you."

"You don't have to, but I know the truth, and it happened that night she threw a beer bottle at my head."

"She did what? How come you haven't told anyone this?"

"Because it missed and hit my arm instead. I still have the scar to prove it."

The truth is looking at that old photo is worse than mom cheating on daddy cause it reminds me of the wonderful life I lost. I miss that life. What happened to us?

Nikki B

Chapter 17

I came from my doctor's appointment and Doctor Green said things were looking good with the twins, and that I'm healthy. He wanted me to walk more and get more exercise since I'm at the end of my seventh month.

Mary and my mother tried to explain to me how important exercise is, and how it would make the delivery easier. Once I told Charles he said that he was happy that we only have two more months to go.

I wrote Sam and told him all about my doctor appointments, and when he wrote back he said that he was happy for me. I was really upset because I wanted him there to see the birth of my children.

Now that the time was almost near. I decided that it was time for me to drop into Kevin's room and start to use some of the money he left.

I got up off the bed, which was super hard being seven months pregnant with twins, and walked over, to my bookcase where I placed the letter along with the note Kevin left me.

When I reached behind it I didn't feel anything. I started to panic and pushed the bookcase out and was shocked to see that it was gone. I started to pull all my books down and empty out all of my dressers but couldn't find a single trace of my little box.

"MARY!!!!MARTIN! HAVE YOU SEEN A LITTLE BLACK BOX ANYWHERE!?!?!?!" I asked them rushing down the stairs, and I nearly fell. Luckily Martin was there to catch me.

"Martin have you seen my little black box. Please tell me you seen it." I asked out of breath.

"I think I seen Mary with one. Does it have a heart craved into the sided and a picture of you and Kevin?"

"Yes it does."

"Well I saw Mary walking with it to her room. She said something about your mother trying to open it."

"Where is she now?"

"I think she is still in her room."

I thanked him with a hug and a kiss and ran off to Mary's room. As I gotten close to Mary's room I heard the sound of jazz music. I could also smell the sweet smell of chocolate. I walked up to her door and opened it enough to look in.

Mary's room was filled with pictures of me and Kevin along with our parents' marriage photos on one side of the room and on the other were pictures of her kids and family.

"Are you being a little sneak,

Aaliyah baby? Please don't tell me you are turning into your mother." Mary said as she walked up behind me.

I jumped and turned to see Mary in her black and white maids outfit. She was only 52, but she had the body figure of a 24 year old. *'How does she keep her body looking so good?'* I would never know.

"Well..I..mmmmmm....Mary   I'm sorry I thought you were in your room." I told her as I scratched my head.

She laughed at me and pushed me into her room. "Here you go baby cakes." she handed me the black box and I hugged it tightly.

I was so happy to have my box back but I wanted to know more about her family.

"Those are my children, God how I miss them." She said when she saw me looking at their photos.

As she talked I couldn't believe it. I use to feel like we kept Mary from her family, but she had photos of our family right next to hers. I used to believe that we stole her from them and told her so.

"No you didn't. I choose to stay because someone had to raise you and apparently it wasn't going to be your mama. I love you as if you were my own child."

Nikki B

*C*hapter 18

This morning as I was getting ready for school, I started to feel a sharp pain. It wasn't bad at first, but when the next one hit me it made me fall to my knees. I started to call out for Mary, but I remembered that she and Martin left for the week and that she called her friend, Roxanna, to come watch over us.

"ROXANNA! ROXANNA!" I called out.

Five minutes had passed before Roxanna appeared at my door. She was a little woman standing at least 5'1. She had jet black hair and the features of a young woman, but she was the same age as Mary.

"What's wrong sweetie pie?" She asked as she helped me off the floor and unto the bed.

I grabbed onto her shirt and said through pain that I thought the baby was coming early. I saw the look of panic on her face as she ran to the phone in the hallway and called 911.

Once that round of pain stopped, I reached across my bed and picked up my cell to call Charles.

"Damn, Aaliyah what's so important that you needed to wake me up for?" He asked into the phone.

"I THINK THE BABY IS COMMING!" I yelled back at him.

I could tell he was getting out of the bed as the call ended because I heard him hit his leg or something on the side of the dresser.

Roxanna came back inside the room

and said that the ambulance would be here in a little while. I started to cry as the pain continued, and it wasn't long before I could hear the sounds of the sirens outside of the house. They asked me a few questions before they loaded me up and drove me to the nearest hospital.

About twenty minutes after I arrived Charles and Ms. Parker walked in.

"Aaliyah, are you alright?" He asked as he sat next to my bed.

He looked down at me while pushing my hair out of my eyes.

"Yea I'm cool now the doctor gave me something to stop the contractions. He said that it wasn't time yet."

"Well thank God it wasn't anything serious. Charles nearly broke my hip trying to get me out of the house." Ms. Parker said.

I laughed as Charles started to blush.

"But that's not all." I said.

"It's not what else could it be.

You're not in labor anymore."

"Well the doctor said he's keeping me here until the babies are due next month."

Ms. Parker eyes widened. "The babies are due next month? Man, how time flies." She said as she sat down in the chair on the opposite side of me.

"Well it's not moving fast enough for me. These babies are killing me. I'm so glad that they are due soon.

While me and Ms. Parker was talking Charles slowly pushing back the cover that was covering my huge belly. Once his hand touched my belly, the babies jumped.

"Oh man I think they both jumped when I touched you." He said proudly.

The room got quiet. Ms. Parker looked at Charles. "Yes they do that something."

Charles slowly rubbed my belly and asked. "Are they sure that the babies are alright Aaliyah?"

"Yes baby they are alright. Both of them are. You don't have to worry, I'm in good hands."

"That's good I don't want nothing to go wrong.".

"I just wish Sam was here for the birth of our babies."

"He will be out of jail before you know it."

He would say anything to help keep her calm. Yes he loved his brother but he loves Aaliyah more.

Nikki B

C*hapter 19*

I was beginning to get tired of lying around in bed. I looked out of the window and got a little sad. It was a beautiful day yet I was stuck here. I flipped through the TV channels hoping that something would catch my interest but nothing did so I decided to go to sleep.

The sound of screaming woke me up. It was coming from the room across the hall from me. I talked to the lady a few times since I've been here. Her name was Rocelle Lewis, and she was in her early 30's and she was giving birth to her third child. We talked a lot when I first got here and I learned a lot about her too. She's a teacher at my grandfather's school and was glad to meet me.

I slowly got out of bed and walked across the hall; the sound of her screaming and cursing out her husband echo through the halls.

I looked from her to her husband and he looked like he wasn't listening to her, but he was watching the birth. She looked over and saw me peeking inside her room.

"Aaliyah, come here and hold my hand sweetheart."

I was scared but wanted to see a life being brought into the world so I did as I was told and grabbed on to her hand. She had a tight grip and wouldn't let go, but I didn't mind.

After 15 minutes of screaming, cursing, and the doctor's endless 'push' speech, Danny Leo Lewis was born. She allowed me to hold him and for the first time since I became pregnant I actually felt like a mother, and the feeling alone made me wanna cry.

I held him as long as I could, but as soon as I walked back to my room my tears started to fall.

I kept that moment in mind as I fell to asleep, but I was awaken by the feeling of someone slowly rubbing my face. I didn't open my eyes but just leaned into the persons touch. Their hands were soft and felt as if an angel was trying to calm me down.

"Wake up Aaliyah. Come on, wake up."

As soon as they spoke I knew it had to be no one but Diana. I opened my eyes and smiled. Diana had grown since the last time I seen her.

"Awww, you looked so peaceful when you sleeping. I didn't even want to wake you." she said as she gently starts to rub and my belly.

I don't know if I had fallen back to

141

sleep or what, because now I could hear more people talking.

"OMG!!!!!! You have gotten so big I haven't seen you since we were 7." Maya said.

When I opened my eyes tI saw Maya, Tina, Sasha, and Dainel. Tina was sitting next to me; Sasha was standing up at the foot of my bed. Maya and Diana were standing in the door way, and Dainel was holding a food tray as he walked over to my bed. He wasn't paying too much attention to me but he did manage to get the tray to the little table stand near Sasha.

The look she gave him showed that she didn't approve of him staring at her the way he was. Tina looked down at me and smiled.

"She's awake guys. You look so beautiful when you sleep."

"So I was told." I **giggled** as she made the cutest blush.

Diana looked over at me and

smiled. My God I swear she has gotten taller since I saw her a few years back, but I was so happy that she came.

We weren't talking but a few minutes before we heard a knock at the door.

"May I come in please?"

"Yea." Maya said eye-balling the door like she can see right through it.

The door opened with a slow pace and in came a little girl with a big white bow in her hair.

"I'm sorry to bother you but my name is Oliva Johnson. I have been coming by your room a lot while you were asleep. I know it sounds creepy, but I thought you looked very beautiful while you slept." Her face was getting redder and redder as she talked, "You reminded me of my mommy when she was pregnant with my little brother and I was just wondering......" she said.

She held her head down and got quiet. She stood there quietly and slowly shaking. I shifted in my bed in an attempt to get up. Diana noticed my poor attempt and helped me. I walked over to the little girl and grabbed her hand. She was a bit surprised by my sudden moment and tensed up a bit but she kept her head down.

"It's ok sweetie. Can I borrow your hand for a moment?" I asked her.

She slowly nodded as I lifted her hand and pressed it against my stomach.

"Can you feel them?" I asked her the moment she raised her head. "Can you feel their little kicks?" I asked her as she rubbed her little hand around my stomach.

"How many are there in your tummy?" She asked me as she pulled her hand away.

"It's two of them a boy and a girl." I told her as I held my hand out so that she could that it. She grabbed my hand and I slowly walked back to my bed.

I got back into bed and left a space for her. She climbed in with a little help from Diana. I offered her some of the food that the hospital had given me. She gladly accepted it.

"So, you come by to watch Aaliyah sleep. Is that like an everyday thing or a once in a while thing?" Maya asked her.

"It's almost an everyday thing, but when I can't come over here. I ask one of the nurses to take a picture of her so I can draw her. Doesn't she look like Sleeping Beauty?" Oliva said as if it was perfectly normal.

"Wait are you a patient here?" Tina asked.

"Yes. I have cancer. They found me a donor and I will be having surgery sometime this month."

"Poor girl."

I heard Dainel say as Sasha cried in his arms. Sasha is always a sucker for little kids with problems. It's one of the reasons she is trying so hard to become a doctor so she can help children like Oliva.

I placed my hand on Oliva's

shoulder and gave her a hug.

"How old are you sweetie?" I asked her as her little hands wrapped around my side.

"I'm 7 years old. You hug me just like my mommy use to and your hair is soft like hers too."

I felt sorry for her.

"Where are your parents? What happened to them?"

She bowed her head and began to cry a little. "My mommy left me and my brother at the train station. We called our daddy but when he came he only picked up my brother and left me sitting on the sidewalk. I stayed at an orphanage for years until I saw my father but he was with another woman and 2 older children a boy and girl."

"Do you have a picture of your father?"

She pulled out a picture.

"Yes here. This the only one of him I got."

She handed me the picture and I nearly had a heart attack. The man in her picture looked exactly like my father. .

Nikki B

*C*hapter 20

It's been a month since I found out I had a little sister and brother, but that's not what hurt me. It's the fact that my father had cheated on my mom. I thought that my mom was the slutty hoe, but my father turned out to be a no good dad to some poor kid.

"I hope you aren't thinking about Oliva." Charles said as he moved around on the bottom of the bed.

"Yes I am, but I can't figure out is where the boy at? Why did he only pick up the boy? Why did he leave them? Why did......"

I tried to finish but Charles put his finger over my mouth. "You know you ask too many questions?" He said as he placed a soft kiss on my cheek. It made me blush a little. He smiled. "Awwww! How cute. You're blushing."

I quickly pushed him off of the bed and pulled the sheet over my face.

"Ow! That hurt love. I think I might cry." Charles teased.

I uncovered my face a little to see his big goofy smile.

"Apparently you are not hurt that bad." We heard a voice say from the doorway.

We both looked to see Victoria, Charles big sister on his father side, standing there with a big smile.

"Oh! Hey Victoria how are you?" I asked as she walked over to my bed.

"Hey sis. What are you doing here?" Charles asked as he got up off of the floor.

"Just came by to check on my new

little sister and my niece and nephew."
She said as she placed her hand on
Charles head.

Charles made a face that showed
he was happy to have his sister here. "Oh
and there is someone else here to see
you Aaliyah come on in." She said as she
walked over to the door.

I watched the door open. Finally it
opened wide enough and a tall figure
stepped in.

"Hey there Aaliyah darling." Sam
said with a wide smile.

"I'm so happy to see you Sam. How
did..... I mean who......" I tried to say but
the words got stuck. I was just happy to
have Sam back in my life.

"Your mom dropped the changes
against me. She told them that she was
mistaken. I don't know how she pulled it
off but I'm glad."

"Good at least she did one good
thing out of her life for me."

"Tell me about it." Charles replied

as he walked over and gave his brother a hug.

***

Later that week my mom came by to see me alone with my dad. It was around the time that Oliva usually comes to visit me. When they walked in, Oliva was sitting in the bed with her wheelchair close by.

The nurse didn't mind her being over here. They said it was good for her recovery. They were also happy that her surgery was a complete success. It's been a week since her surgery and she has healing very quickly.

"Hey dear." My mom says as she stared down at Oliva, who was eating my little cup of vanilla pudding.

"I had been better mom. Oh and this is......." before I could even get her name out, my dad hugs Oliva.

"Oliva my sweet princess why are you here?" he said as she hugged him back.

"Wait a minute. How do you know this girl?" My mother asked with an angry tone.

"Oh Daddy!" Oliva said. "I had cancer, and I was in so much pain. Why didn't you get me like you did Jason? Why did you leave me?"

"I'm sorry sweetie Daddy couldn't get you that time. There was so much going on and I knew I couldn't take you home with me."

"So my brother doesn't live with you?"

"No, sweetie he doesn't. I tried to find you."

"It's okay can we be a family now daddy; me, you, Jason and Aaliyah. Please daddy please?" Oliva said as she grabbed my arm and pulled me into a hug with my father.

My mom wasn't happy about this and walked out of the room. For the first time my father showed signs that he didn't care what my mother thought.

"Yes Oliva we can. Now we had two new additions to our little family Aaliyah; Oliva, and Jason Johnson."

"So that means you're going to go get Jason dad?" I asked him.

No one was happier than I am now that my brother and sister would be safe and well taken care of.

***

Since Sam's release he and Charles have stayed by my side; it felt just like old times. I watched as Sam laid slept in the chair over by the window and Charles laid on the little sofa that he claimed was too hard and uncomfortable for any human to sleep on. Every time he would start to complain about that thing, I would tell him to try laying on his back with two babies inside his stomach on an uncomfortable metal bed and tell me which was worse.

He would always smile and tell me maybe the little sofa wasn't that bad. Looking at the two loves of my life in the same room made me a bit calm about giving birth. Maybe it wounld't hurt as bad as I thought it would. Not with these two by my side.

It was about three am on June 20, 2012, when I felt the first wave of pain. The pain was so bad that I felt like I wanted to die. My scream woke up Sam and made Charles fall off of the little sofa.

"What in the world?" Charles said as he got off of the floor.

"The babies are coming! Call the doctor, nurse, or somebody!" I yelled at him.

His eyes widen as he pushed the button for the nurse. The nurse came running in and Charles called my parents and Ms. Parker letting them know that the babies were on their way.

I laid there screaming until the doctor arrived and gave me something for the pain. I couldn't have them naturally so I laid there looking up at the ceiling while being wheeled into the operation room.

I held Charles hand while he was telling me what was going on. Then I heard the sound of one of the babies.

"It's a girl." Charles said full of joy.

Two minutes later I heard the sound of my son. Once the children were born all I wanted to do was hold them, but the looks on Charles face while he was holding our daughter that I didn't won't to break up there bonding. And when I saw Sam he was holding our son with the same look of joy on his face.

"Oh Aaliyah, they are beautiful; do you want to figure out whose babies they are?"

"No I already know whose they are." I said looking over at Charles.

"Then whose are they?" My mother asked.

"They are Charles and that's the end of it."

Sam looked at me.

"That's right! They are my brother kids so there is no need for a DNA test.

This is Charles family and I will be the best uncle ever." Sam said as he placed a kiss on top of his nephew little head.

"Now that that's settled. We have to name them." Charles said while placing our daughter into my arms.

"I think that I'll name the boy Charles Juniors and the girl should be named Samantha after Sam. What do you think?"

Sam looked at me with surprise in his eyes.

"Oh Aaliyah you didn't have to do that."

"No big brother it's an honor to name our daughter after you."

Not too long after that my mom gave birth to my new little brother William Damien Jackson. After his birth my father had a blood test done. I guess he wasn't as forgiving as me. After the results were read and he found out that the baby wasn't his, he filed for a divorce. He said that he didn't blame my mother but there was just too much cheating going on between the both of them and they were better off apart.

After I went home Charles asked my father if he and Sam could move in so they could help me raise the children. He allowed it after he put down a few ground rules.

When my mother heard about that she went off, which caused her a big custody battle concerning baby William and me. To make a long story short my father won the case and got full custody of William and the judge ruled my mom an unfit mother. In the end, she was lucky to even have visitation rights. My dad was glad that he got custody of William. He said he loved him even when he found out that he wasn't his.

GANGSTA KILLERS

The Betrayal

By Author: Veronica Meek

Chapter 1

Mike

As I opened my eyes slowly pain shot from the front all the way to the back of my head. It took a moment for my sight to begin to clear. I looked around trying to figure out just where I was, but the only thing I saw was a big bay window. When I looked out; all I saw was rain hitting heavy on the window pane.

The room was dark; the only light was coming from the street lights below. I tried to listen for a sound, any sound, but all I heard was the pouring rain.

I closed my eyes again hoping that something would come back to me, but everything was foggy. I couldn't remember anything so I begin to panic, and for the life of me I didn't know why. Why am I so scared? Why am I here in this cold dark place? I couldn't help but ask myself that question over and over again, but in the end I still came up with no answer. It was clearly easy to see that I was lying inside of a hospital room.

I looked down hoping to see a name tag or something that could at least tell me who I am. When I tried to move my hands that's when I noticed that I was bound; then I heard a clinking sound as the cuffs hit the side of the bedrails.

Now panic really set in. Why was I handcuffed to the bed? What could I have done for me to end up like this? My heart started to race and the monitors begin to sound off. Oh God am I having a heart attack? It shows feels like it. Sweat begins to pour from my body as my head begins to pound.

My room door flew open as doctors and nurses came running inside. There were people everywhere. Some were pushing buttons on the machines while others tried to work on me. I couldn't speak. I could hear them asking me questions; but I couldn't get any words out.   "Mr. Crawford you really need to calm down." The doctor said while leaning over me.

If I could calm down don't they think that I would have done so by now? My chest is killing me. Oh God I'm dying. I just know I am.

"Mr. Crawford I'm going to ask you some questions please try to answer if you can it's very important. Do you understand me?"

I tried to reply, but I still couldn't get any words out. So I nob my head "yes" showing that I understood.

"Good now listen to me Mr. Crawford; I really need you to try to calm down everything is going to be alright. You have to get your emotions under control. I know it's scary waking up and not knowing where you are. But you have to believe me we'll only here to help you."

I tried to lift my hands up again showing her that I wanted to know why I'm handcuffed to the bed.

She looks down. "That's was for your safety Mr. Crawford. You kept pulling out your IV's, but now that you're awake we can removed them. You see you been here for a while, but first I want to know do you remember what happened to you."

I shook my head no. I'm more confused now then I was when I first open my eyes.

"Then I'm going to explain things as best as I can."

I shook my head yes once again, because I was more than ready to know what happened to me and why was I here. There is one good thing that came out of this attack; I learned my last name.

"I'm going to start from the beginning. On November 23 you were brought here for multi gunshots to your chests and you were also shot once in the head. You are a very lucky young man. Tell me Mr. Crawford do you remember anything about that or what happened to you?"

"No!" I even surprised myself when I answered her question.

"Do you know your name?"

"No I don't doctor. I can't remember a damn thing." I said angrily.

"It's okay Mr. Crawford that's a normal reaction from someone that has brain trauma. The good news is that most of the swelling is gone, but you still have a long way to go."

"How long have I been here?" My voice sounded as weak as I felt.

"You have been here a little over two months."

"Two months!"

I watched as the doctor sat down on the edge of the bed; lifted my hands up and removed the cuffs. She looked at me and smiled. I just couldn't help but to relax a little more. The shock I was in was all but gone except for the headache that was pounding like a drum. She has a way to make a man forget everything even the pain that was pounding in my head.

"Would you like something for the pain? I noticed that you keep rubbing the side of your head."

"Yes I would love something thank you. Can you answer something else for me doctor?"

"Sure what is it?"

"What is my first name?" I tried to smile but the pain was unbearable.

"It's Mike, but that is enough for today. I'm going to leave you to get some more rest. So someone would be back to give you something for the pain. Tomorrow we'll have a lot to talk about before I call the police and let them know that you're awake."

"Thank you doctor that means a lot to me and maybe by then I would have remembered more about what happened."

"Mike don't try to rush your memory it would come back in time; rushing it would only cause more headaches. Just relax and get some sleep."

"Don't you think I been sleeping enough DR?" I smiled.

"Yes, but the more you rest and sleep the better your chances of healing and getting your memory back."

I closed my eyes as she walked out the room, and I didn't even bother to open them back up when I heard the door open and close again. I could hear the nurse moving around getting everything she needed together.

"Mr. Crawford we'll have you feeling better in no time." The nurse said.

Whatever she gave me put me out in minutes. I didn't even hear her when she left the room.

Cory

I treated today like any other day. I made my rounds, check my supply's, and headed down to see my big brother. The months seem to move slowly waiting on Mike to wake up. So I was more than happy to receive the phone call from the hospital informing me that Mike had waking from his coma.

I knew that my brother was lucky to be alive, and I prayed to God every day that he would save him even though he has taken so many lives his self. The work we do is deadly and Mike paid the price for slipping. It damn near ended his life.

I don't know what I would ever do if I lost one of my brothers, because it has always been the three of us. No one looked after Isaiah and I like Mike have and now it's our turn to repay the favor. Since the day he was shot I have had my ear to the streets trying to find out who was responsible. Lately I felt like I'm very close to figuring it out, but only Mike can tell me the truth.

I hate watching him waste away in that hospital bed. He isn't anything, but skin and bones now. It wasn't like he was a very big man just tall has hell. He was the one to turn too when you needed a job done. Isaiah and I learned from the best; no one could ever take his place. It was like watching one of the mighty God's fall.

I looked over at my ole girl sitting next to me in the car. She wanted nothing more than for me to step into Mike's shoes. Jamaya just didn't know the bond my brother's and I have. I had to listen to her go on and on about who should be the one running our family now, but it's only one head of this family and that's Mike. How could I get her to understand that? It's like whatever I say goes in one ear and out the other. The bitch is just money hungry; I knew that and always have since day one.

There is one good thing I can say about Jamaya. She's a ride and die chick. No matter how money hungry she is she has always had my back; from the beginning until now. I just hate to let her down, but Mike is our boss and she just has to understand that.

"Cory did they say how long Mike been awake?" Jamaya asked.

"No, but I don't care he's woke now. I'm happy to be able to look into my bro face and finally get some answers."

"Yeah, thanks to you he would be able to walk right back in on top. I told your ass to step up and now it's too late."

Before I know what happened I had her by the neck damn near pulled her out of her seat sideways.

"Jamaya I telling you this for the last fucking time Mike is the head of this family. Don't make me have to say this shit again, because to be honest this is getting tiresome."

I never seen her cry before, it surprised me that her eyes started to fill with tears. I hate hurting her so it made me loosen my grip.

"Why do you always do this baby? You always make me hurt you."

It was hard to let her go; sometimes she just pushes all the wrong bottoms. She tried to smile, but she was shaken so badly. I could tell she wasn't happy that I still haven't let her go. Sometimes she makes me just want to kill her. I only released her when my cell rang. I heard her butt hit the car seat; she was trying hard to pull in some much needed air.

"Speak. Yeah I'm on my way now thanks for the update Dr."

I looked over at Jamaya when I hung up the phone. She was trying not to look at me, and she still hard tears falling down her face.

"Baby come here." I pulled her by the arm and eased her close to me. She didn't even try to resist. "I'm sorry baby you know I don't like hurting you, but you just don't know when to stop. This is my bro you keep talking about. I wouldn't be a man if I continued to let you disrespect him like that. You feel me?"

I felt her head shaking yes on my chest. I knew then I had finally gotten my message across. Why did it have to take all that for her to understand the loyalty between me and my brothers? Why do I have to damn near beat it through her head?

"Baby I love you; you know that so please stop crying."

"I love you too baby; I'm sorry. I always find ways of pissing you off." She said sniffing.

"Yeah that you do." I laughed. "I didn't have a right to put my hands on you though." I kissed her on her forehead and let her lay there a few seconds more. She felt good in my arms. This is one of the moments that I hate to let her go. "Okay baby now we have to get to the hospital."

We made the ride to South Side Hospital in total silence. I looked over at her, and saw she was busy fixing her makeup. At that moment she had put her brink wall back up. She hated to show signs of weakness, but mostly I did too. I reached down and turned on the CD player and let Gucci Mane do his thing.

She reaches over and picked up her matching pair of Dolce Gabbana sunglasses as we headed down Upper Riverdale Road. I watched the same houses going the same route and it seems like I made this trip a thousand times; this time it seems a lot easier.

Isaiah

As soon as I pulled the trigger blood flew on my brand new Jordan's. Damn I hate messing up my shit, because I never know when I'll have somewhere else to go. Like today I'm heading to see my brother and this damn fool just leaked all over me. Maybe I need to start wrapping plastic bags around my shoes. Hell even goes as fast as putting on a jump suit in that case. I laughed to myself.

The sound of moaning brought me back to reality. I looked down at this fool trying hard not to die. What I need to do damn new blow his head off.

"Fool just die!" I said aloud.

He looked up at me with glazed eyes. I could tell he was hanging on with as much life I had in my little finger. I give him credit he really putting up a fight; holding on to every last minute. Damn fool. I pointed the gun and shot once again.

I guess he believed that I might have had some kind of heart. What he doesn't know is I'm heartless as they come. Sometimes I believe I'm the worse out of the three of us. Don't get me wrong I don't mind. I don't care about being a cold hearted killer. It's in my blood; it's just part of my nature. If my brother's wasn't walking this earth I wouldn't give a damn about nobody.

I looked down at my shoes again and headed to my truck shaking my head. Lucky for me I just went and grabbed another pair from Greenbrier this morning. I hit the button and the locks sounded off in the quiet neighborhood. I looked around knowing there has to be a bag somewhere in here to put these shoes in. As soon as I saw it I pulled it out, and slide out of my shoes. My feet hit the cold ground and a chill went right up my spine.

I pulled out my new pair of J's and ease my foot inside; grabbing the box and gas can I walked back over to the body. This is the part of the job I hate. I should just leave this nigga right here. I hate the smell of a burning body. When I open up the gas can and started to pour the smell of gas was strong. I took a second and pulled out the matches. After striking it I dropped it down on the body. In a matter of seconds the body went up in flames. I took the box with the shoes inside and added it to the growing flames. Just for good measure I poured a little more gas to keep the fire burning hot.

The flames were sky high now; the best part about my surroundings is that not one soul could see it. I stood there watching as the flames dance across the empty buildings. I watched as the fire burned until there was nothing left. It didn't take that long he wasn't bigger than a ten year old boy. That's what Rico gets for trusting a small as man. They ain't shit.

Mike has always told us never trust a man if he isn't at least 5'7. The smaller they are the sneakier they are. Some of them hard legs just want learn. That's that reason they sent people like me and my brother's after them.

Our circle is small and only the best is allowed to do what we do; we better not even get word of someone else around here doing hits in Atlanta. That's our department. If they want to continue to pull air through their lungs they best to find another business.

I heard sounds of dogs in the background. It wasn't good to hang around the crime scene for too long. I don't care how far away from the city it is. My mind went back to Mike and my heart froze over again. I just couldn't believe we almost lost him; the streets are lucky we didn't, because that would have opened up the gates of hell.

I felt myself getting angry about the whole situation again. I really need to learn how to control the anger I have inside of me. First, of all it isn't good for business; it damn show isn't good for me; but I have always been a hot head. That's what Mike always calls me. It put a smile of my face, because I know the first thing he's going to say as soon as he sees me…"I know you haven't been out there being a hot head Isaiah."

Don't know one knows me better than him so it's not going to be a reason to lie. It's who I am; nothing going to change that.

My drive back to the city did wonders for me. I was at ease; nearly at peace with myself, and that's a good thing. Mike knows when I'm on some crazy shit.

With me being in the middle of Mike and Cory it's like I have to work even harder to please both of them. They both seem to have their own things going on, and I'm left to keep the peace. It just surprised me that Cory hasn't tried to step up and take Mike's place. It's been plenty of times I've overheard that no good as bitch of his in his ear trying to full his head with it. I told that boy Jamaya ain't know good, but when you're in love you don't hear anything anyone trying to tell you.

I'm not going to keep thinking about that; it isn't going to do nothing but stress me right back out. I don't need that. I can't wait to see my bro man it seems like forever since I looked in his eyes.

With that in mind I floored it. I know I'm pushing the speed limits, but today is a good day; tickets be damn. I pasted car after car pushing my Yukon to the limit. Even going ninety miles she still rides smooth as hell. I love this truck. I flew in and out of traffic blowing my horn driving like a mad man. I finally felt my blood start to warm from the excitement of the ride. I finally feel a little human. That's what I live for the thrill of the chase.

THE LYRICIST FIRM

PRESENTS

Love
Or
Death

By: Lynnett Fox

Mi Vida Loca

I woke up dazed and confused. What happened last night? My head is fucking pounding and I'm hanging like a mother fucker. I feel like I got introduced to a Louie and he won the slug fest. I can't see strait and I feel like I'm about to throw up. Damn what did I do last night? I sure hope I didn't get myself into some shit again. I was known to get too wasted and start popping off. I just prayed this was not one of those times.

Suddenly I'm startled at the light sound of snoring coming from beside me. *"Shit! How the hell did I end up in bed with this cobrone?"* Okay now? Let me piece together the events of the night before. Eee I remember my home girls picking me up, we were headed to a party with these fine ass vato's we had met earlier in the day. We were all looking fine as fuck; dolled out as my friend Gorda's dad said as we were leaving her house.

We went to a house party on 5th and Corona. Not many people were there but we were having fun. We were drinking on 40's and playing beer pong. I remember that and also losing my ass at it too. I was flirting with a few of the homeboys. It's starting to come back to me, but my head pounding like a jackhammer. I remember dancing with this one guy. I thought about looking over to see if it was him but I'm scared what if it's one of the ugly friends? Aww shit why do I do these things? Okay come on I know I can remember, I was dancing and drinking then I went to the back room.

Oh yes its cloudy but I'm beginning to remember.... I shake my head in disgust. I need to get my ass a "wake up" if I was going to make it through the day. I needed some energy and I needed it quick. I needed something to take the edge off. I started to look around the room still not looking at the person lying beside me. I was too scared at who it might be. I started a silent laugh as I thought of that movie

Coyote Ugly. You know when the bar owner tells the girl why she named the bar? When a person gets so drunk they wake up and want to gnaw their arm off to get away.

I was happy when I looked on the table to my right and there was a shiny pile of white powder. I grabbed the straw made two generous lines put the straw by my nostril and inhaled one line, switched nostrils and snorted the other. *"Awwww, nothing like snorting my "Folgers" in the morning. It's good till the last drop."* I laugh with that thought. I lean back, finally looking at the dude sound asleep beside me. He was sweating all kinds, which grossed me out. How was it; that I always ended up with the pendejo's of the group? He wasn't ugly but he sweats to damn much. That too me was the mark of an alcoholic or addict. And I was neither of them. I just attracted them it seemed. But I did have to admit I always ended up with "the supplier" shit I knew who to go to I wasn't no dumb ass.

Here I was 20 years old, had graduated high school (promised my abuella that I would do at least that) and here I am lying next to some chulo who I didn't even remember his name. Speaking of names, you're probably wondering what's mine, Well I'm "Weda" yes I know that means white girl, well I come from a brown beautiful Chicana mother, and a white good for nothing sperm donor supposed to be father. I say sperm donor loosely because the only thing he ever did was knock my mama up, give me his white DNA and name and then he split, leaving my mom to fend for herself.

She was only 16 when she had me she had a rough life, fucking bastard. My government name is Christina Thomas; yeah I know not exactly the greatest name to have when you live in the barrio. I always wanted my mom's name Sanchez but she wouldn't let me use it. I know I need to be proud of both my heritages, but how can a chika be happy with a culture she knows nothing about? I grew up in the "Hood". My familia is my mom, my Abuelita, my Tia Angela (my mom's little sister), little Nicolas and my girls.

Me and my home girls had been through a lot together, I've known them since we was in preschool, from singing grease songs on the playground with Angelo Vega, all the way through high school and then some. My clique was the shit. We got jumped in just like the vato's. We all fucked each other up till we couldn't stand. I mean there wasn't enough of us to be "our" own girl gang, but we were down with the Ese's so they had accepted the 4 of us as part of them.

My girls...
Sandra "Sad Eyes" Martinez
Lupe "Gorda" Romero
Angel "Giggles' Cervantes

Sad eyes always looked sad. We use to tease her that she looked like someone had peed in her cheerios, but if you had grown up the way sad eyes did, you'd be sad too. From the time she could walk some "uncle" or relative was always putting their hands on her. Her family had been a bunch of pervs. She left home last year. Sandra was pretty but always down played it deciding she didn't "like" men and liked women instead.

We didn't judge her for it either, she was our sister and we loved her. Sad eyes had been with the same girl for like 3 years, and that's longer than any of us had been dating any vato. Her girlfriend was a butch bitch named "Loca" she was fucking crazy that's for sure. She took on dudes in fights and was way protective over sad eyes, but she loved her and that was very evident. You could just see how those two were so in love with each other. Even if it was weird to all of us, you know two girls; it worked for them so we all just rolled with it. Sad Eyes lived with Loca so she could only go out with the home girls when Loca was at work.

Now Gorda she was the "fighter" of our group. She had four older brothers who were all OG's and they expected her to be just as hard as they were. She was a full-fledged member of our set, The Los Cornales. She rode on drive byes, fought chika's, and vatos; sometimes at the same time. Lupe's family had been generational to the barrio and to the familia. Gorda like her name says was a big girl, but she had a pretty face. She carried herself well too. She could do hair good and always had it some flashy way. She was a fighter yet she was still all girl. I know I didn't want to piss her off at all. I looked up to her mom and dad. I even called them that. They were my second parents. Gorda's brothers were all cool as hell.

Now me and Angel had a sort of love hate relationship going on. I'm the one who had given her the nickname "Giggles" back in the 6th grade. She was the only person I could truly talk too. Well lately anyways. She was funny as fuck and always had my ass laughing. She was silly and corny, but I loved her. We had our share of fights but we worked through them. She was my partner in crime.

Giggles were thin almost anorexic with dark hair and dark skin. Guys seemed to like her. My mom said she felt sorry for Angel, she said she was a homely girl who got guys for being easy. As you see my mom didn't like her. She didn't like any of my friends for that matter she said all they did was use me for my car and money and get me into trouble. I didn't need any help getting myself into trouble. That was something that just came natural.

Well "my friend" had woken up and wanted to get back to where we had left off the night before. He begins kissing the back of my neck and I swear I felt like gagging because his breath stank so badly. It was like a cross between beer, onion and garlic. He reached over and grabbed the straw and divided the powder into four rows. Took his in and kissed my mouth real hard. This was the part of this shit that I did not like.

All of them were the same to if you wanted to be included in the party you had to play by their rules. I knew the game and as long as I didn't want to pay for my candy I would have to play along. We kissed for a few minutes; thank God I didn't throw up. He then handed me the straw and let me do my lines. He spoke real soft.

"Weda, you know your one fine ass rouka? I want to spread a line across your titties and get you all tingly then spread one across my dick and you can lick that shit clean."

"Well then come on papi," I whisper in my sexiest voice.

I pulled my beater over my head with my 36 c's popping out and perky. I'm a good girl and I always do as I'm told. You'd think I would be ashamed right? After all God knows what I had did the night before, so I just went with the flow. He laid a line across my nipple and began to lick and nibble on them. I immediately became wet. That's what the coke did for me; made me horny as fuck. I moaned for him not to stop.

"Oh papi you feel so good."

"Oh you like that mami don't you?"

"Yes papi you're making me feel all tingly inside."

He then begins to play with my pussy first slowly then faster and faster bringing two fingers inside me while using his thumb to caress my clit. I was getting wetter and wetter just as I was about to cum he jumped up, got a weird look in his eyes.

"You got to go Weda, get dressed and chale." He says.

Here we go; I rolled my eyes and giggled inside and again did as I was told these fucking dealers were all the same. Once the coke set in they all got paranoid and limp dicked. I was not about to argue with a coked out drug dealer. I knew my cue.

"Thanks for the party," I tell him as I got dressed and was on my way.

These puto's were all alike get some blow in them and they couldn't do shit. They'd all get fidgety looking out the windows. Sometimes they would make you stay on the ground for hours without making a sound because they were so paranoid. They always were thinking the hooda was coming for them. I took what I could get from them; see these pendejos were so stupid; I always took a pinch when they weren't looking. And no it's not what you're thinking I DON'T have a coke problem.

I like to use recreational and at least I wasn't a crack head or a slammer. I didn't sell my ass for dope and if I didn't get any I never went hunting for it. I just indulged a little bit to help me feel good.

As I got in my car I shook my head in disgust. *"They are all the same."* I stopped at Gorda's chante before going home. I hated being home. I disappointed my mom and my Abuela. They had wanted me to go to college and do something more with myself then hang out with the homies and work at the local grocery store. I did hate that job. Part time wasn't cutting it. I needed my own crib so I didn't have to answer to anyone. But at the rate I was going it wasn't going to happen anytime soon. So in the meantime I tried to stay away from home as much as possible.

Gorda was chilling on the sofa smoking a joint with her brother Sleepy. He was dreamy. I had been in love with that vato for years, but he only thought of me as a kid sister. He was over 6 ft. tall with his head shaved bald tats all over. He was sexy as hell his body looked like a boxer. He lifted weights all the time with his brothers.

Sleepy was hard core and dangerous he made my panties wet just thinking about him. With his dark eyes and dimples oh how I loved his smile.

"So how was last night?" Gorda asks.

"Aww you know same ole same ole." I tell her as she passed the joint to me.

"Hey Sleepy how have you been? Staying out of trouble?"

"You know me Weda trouble finds me all the time," he says," how are you Mija?"

"I'm okay just maintaining and working."

I took a few hits then told them I was going to their restroom. I needed another wake up. While I lined up two more lines and sniffed them my phone started ringing to NB Ridaz "Until I die" that was Angel's favorite song and her ring tone. Giggles had text that we needed to hook up soon, she had run into this vato we had partied with a few weeks before and he was asking for me; so I text her that I'd be by to pick her up in a couple of hours. I needed to go home and shower the last drug dealer off my body.

Nobody but Angel knew I was into coke. Gorda didn't know cause if she did she'd kick my ass. She was big on how drugs take over the neighborhoods and make people stupid. *"You don't get high you sling it."* Was her motto. So I wasn't about to tell her I used now and then. Gorda was almost as big as Sleepy and I was scared of her.

I stood in the bathroom and chilled for a few minutes then decided to take my happy ass home. I needed to get ready cause me and giggles had a mission to go on. I put my stash back in my bra and looked at myself in the mirror. Had to make sure no powder remnants were left. I said my goodbyes and headed for my ride.